A DARING LADY

"I don't want to live by rules anymore," Eleanor said. "I'm certain I will continue to scandalize everyone just as before. But it will be because I have decided to."

"Bravo," Caldwell said. "I approve of scandalousness. And what is to be your first shocking act? A chip bonnet before Easter? A dinner party without turtle soup?"

"You're horrid," she said in a low voice filled with laughter.

"I am," he agreed readily. He turned to her and found her looking directly at him, her clear eyes distractingly locked with his. "But you must give me credit for living according to your new creed," he said. "I do precisely as I please, damn the consequences. And see how happy I am?"

She thought for a moment, unreadable expressions moving across her face like clouds. "Yes," she murmured at last, as though she was talking to herself. "Damn the consequences."

And with that, she leaned in and kissed him. . . .

BOOKS BY CATHERINE BLAIR

The Scandalous Miss Delaney

The Hero Returns

Athena's Conquest

A Family for Gillian

A Perfect Mismatch

A Scholarly Gentleman

A Viscount for Christmas

A Notorious Lady

Published by Zebra Books

A NOTORIOUS LADY

Catherine Blair

ZEBRA BOOKS
KENSINGTON PUBLISHING CORP.
http://www.kensingtonbooks.com

ZEBRA BOOKS are published by

Kensington Publishing Corp.
850 Third Avenue
New York, NY 10022

All Kensington titles, imprints and distributed lines are available at special quantity discounts for bulk purchases for sales promotion, premiums, fund-raising, educational or institutional use.

Special book excerpts or customized printings can also be created to fit specific needs. For details, write or phone the office of the Kensington Special Sales Manager: Kensington Publishing Corp., 850 Third Avenue, New York, NY 10022. Attn. Special Sales Department. Phone: 1-800-221-2647.

Zebra and the Z logo Reg. U.S. Pat. & TM Off.

First Printing: October 2004
10 9 8 7 6 5 4 3 2 1

Printed in the United States of America

Chapter One

"I don't like this."

John Caldwell looked down at the unknown boy who was bundled to his eyeballs, an expression of bleak misery on the two inches of flesh exposed to the elements. "Why not?" He looked at the boy's sled, then at the snow-covered hill. "Are you scared?"

"Of course not," the boy said scornfully. "I just don't like it."

The child gravely surveyed the busy hillside. Boys and girls were happily tumbling about, quarreling, laughing; in general, behaving like idiots.

Caldwell considered for a fleeting moment suggesting they go down the hill on the sled together. After all, it had been years since he'd indulged in the pleasure, and everyone else was having such a grand time.

A rational voice in his head reminded him that Cambridge University professors did not lower themselves to pastimes such as sledding, and that other people's children were best left to their own devices. He was here merely to find a truant student late for his tutorial session.

Across the top of the ridge, he saw his quarry, Lord Fuller. Fuller, Kittley, and Grenich were dragging up some monstrous contraption made of crates and sled runners. The university students were up to their usual odd starts. Caldwell smiled, hoping they had paid more attention to his astronomy lectures than they had evidently paid to any course of study on engineering or design. Pieces of the conveyance were dropping off like snowflakes.

The professor looked down after a moment to see that the young boy hadn't moved. "What's wrong?" he demanded. "Are you lost? Are you cold?"

The dark eyes, muffled between two scarves and an enormous knit cap, looked at him with despair. "I can't move," he said. "I'm wearing too many clothes."

The boy—perhaps he was seven? Eight? Whelps' ages were a mystery to him—did look something like a pudgy scarecrow, his arms stuck at awkward angles, his neckless head a strange conical shape atop his blue wool coat.

"I suppose that makes it hard to sled," he said. "Particularly if you fell off. Look at that poor fellow there." He pointed to another overdressed creature wallowing like a sow, unable to right himself. "Did your mother dress you like that?"

"Yes. She's worried I might catch cold." A shining row of sweat beads was forming on the boy's forehead. Even just standing there, he was baking like a lobster.

"Here," Caldwell said, unable to watch such misery. "Your mother wasn't accounting for the warmth exertion brings on. You don't need two scarves. And, good Lord, are you wearing two coats as well? Little wonder you haven't fainted yet. Here, leave them here. No, of course no one will take them. I'll mind them for you. Now, isn't that better?"

The boy experimentally waggled his arms. "Much."

John heard a shout and saw that the students' toboggan had already lost a large portion of its midsection before it had even begun its descent. It tottered at the top of the hill, looking very much as though its maiden voyage would be its last.

"Professor Caldwell!" Fuller called. "Dash it all. I missed my tutorial, didn't I? Have you come out here to find me? How dreadful; I'm sorry. But you see, we've built this smashing new thing, and we wanted to try it out."

"Smashing is an appropriate descriptor." Caldwell crossed his arms over his chest, waiting in amusement for the spectacular disaster sure to follow. After a moment, he felt the irritation of distraction and looked down to find that the boy was still standing there beside him, staring blankly down the hill.

"Well?" he said sharply.

"I think you'd better go with me."

Caldwell stared at the boy in surprise for a moment. Children too young to be university students were beyond his experience. They generally had mothers and fathers, nurses and tweenies, tutors and governesses to coddle them.

Seeing no tender parents nearby ready to take on the challenge, he looked down at the sled and abruptly decided there was no harm in it. After all, it would be an excellent excuse for a good run down the hill. He dropped the boy's discarded wrappings in a pile and climbed aboard behind the boy. "Have you sledded before?"

"No. Mama thinks—"

"Well, here we go." He gave them a push with his heels, and they went over the crest of the hill. For a

long, mad, brilliant moment there was nothing but
whiteness, a childish shriek of surprised joy, and tin-
gling sparks of cold. Then their plume of snow
settled, the boy's shouts turned to giggles, and they
plopped over into a drift.

Freed from his woolen fetters, the boy was
quickly on his feet. "That was good," he said in his
peculiar, serious way, as though it had been a job to
be accomplished. "Let's go again."

It had been good. Marvelously cathartic. Sledding should definitely be required of all professors
once in a while. Caldwell was just dusting the snow
out of his hair and wondering where his hat had
gotten to when he saw a gray angel of fury swoop-
ing down upon them.

"William!" the woman exclaimed with such re-
proach and terror that John involuntarily looked
back at the boy to be certain he hadn't missed the
fact that the child had mangled a limb or ruptured
some vital organ on the way down.

"Did you see?" the boy asked. "We went quite fast.
Watch this time while we show you."

"I told you not to go anywhere without me," she
snapped. She gave Caldwell a look that said she
knew good and well he'd intended to abduct the
boy, or at the very least entice him to maim himself
through reckless sledding.

John gave her the impassive cold stare he usually reserved for very unruly students or innkeepers
who did not bring him his ale in good time. "I'm
sorry, madam. Your son asked me to accompany
him."

He surveyed her impartially. Pretty, in a proud
kind of way, and not in the first blush of youth—
perhaps in her late twenties. But her face, high
cheekboned and fine browed, would not have

suited her so much at seventeen. She would have been really quite attractive, if she did not have the air of haughty coldness ridiculously termed breeding.

He preferred merry, saucy girls. Ones who showed their teeth when they laughed, even when they didn't really understand his jokes. Ones who didn't mind, perhaps, a little kiss stolen behind the stairs. Certainly not ones who looked at him with accusatory sparks flying from their humorless gray eyes.

She took the boy possessively by the hand. "Thank you," she said without meaning it at all. "Professor DeVaux is coming. He will help Will if he needs it."

She knew DeVaux? The woman, cold and rigid as an icicle, hardly seemed the type of woman who would attract his fellow astronomy professor. DeVaux had about as much interest in running about after the petticoat set as he did. And he would certainly avoid poker-faced gray shrews like this creature. Though, of course, she might be a friend of his sister's. Or perhaps a relation. After all, DeVaux was a peer and was likely to have all manner of high-in-the-instep kin.

"Where are the rest of your things?" the woman exclaimed. "Where are your blue scarf and the coat from last winter?"

Caldwell was turning away from her motherly tirade when the dark eyes of the boy caught his, beseeching.

"My fault, madam," he interceded. "They are at the top of the hill." He pointed to the dark splotch on the landscape. "The boy was roasting alive in them. It is too much to wrap him up so when he's exercising."

She drew herself up, stiff and straight, her frozen glare stating baldly that she would thank him not to interfere. But instead of wrangling further with him, which he would rather have enjoyed, she turned and marched off, holding her son by the hand, the sled bumping after them like a cowed dog.

He heard a series of wild yells and saw that the homemade toboggan the students had made was now careening down the hill. One of the runners came off immediately, but the bathtub that had evidently made up the primary structure of the contraption continued to slide crossways down the hill.

If anyone was in danger of mangling themselves it was Fuller and his crew. But they were laughing as though they absolutely believed it would be worth it. Caldwell made a mental note to join them on the next run, assuming both they and their creation survived.

"Caldwell," called a voice from the top of the hill. He looked up and saw DeVaux. The man was gesturing for him, so he turned reluctantly from watching the students tumble out of the bathing sled and walked up the hill to his friend.

"I should have known I'd find you here," DeVaux said cheerfully, as they grew close enough to speak. "Always up for a lark, aren't you?" The young professor shook his hand warmly. "Well, it is indeed the perfect day for it. I'm glad I found you. I would like to introduce you to some friends of mine."

Caldwell had a feeling he'd already met them.

DeVaux was a good sort. The best sort, in fact. But he was nonetheless a swell from the left side of London. A viscount, in fact, since his cousin's death last spring, and it stood to reason that the man would have a few lurking high-and-mighty acquaintances from those drawing room days.

He reluctantly followed DeVaux to where the woman in gray was diligently mummifying her son again.

"Eleanor, I'm sorry I was delayed. There is someone I'd like you to meet. Lady Whitcombe, may I introduce you to my colleague, Professor Caldwell? Caldwell teaches astronomy at Trinity with me."

Lady Whitcombe. A grand peeress. Of course she was.

He had the satisfaction of seeing her eyes widen in surprise when she straightened up.

"What a pleasure," he said, with rather sarcastic emphasis. Just because she was a society lady didn't mean he had to grovel.

After a moment's recovery, the woman held out a tiny gloved hand, and he bowed over it. Interestingly, on closer inspection, he could see that her elegant clothes were carefully mended and certainly not the first stare of fashion. He mentally wrote *poor relation sycophanting after DeVaux's blunt* after her name.

"Lady Whitcombe is an old friend. Of the family. That is, just an old friend." DeVaux stumbled slightly, obviously at a loss as to how to introduce her. "And this is her son, William."

"Hello, William." Caldwell amended *relation* to *family friend* and let the epithet stand.

"Hello, sir."

Caldwell was glad to see that the boy was not going to say anything that would reignite the great clothing controversy.

"Eleanor." DeVaux noted for the first time what the woman and her son were doing. "You can't possibly make him wear all those clothes. The exercise will overheat him."

Caldwell resisted the urge to shoot her a naughty grin.

Her perfectly arched brows drew together. "But he is so frail. If he exerts himself too much, it might bring on an inflammation of the lungs."

"Dr. Stalk said he was quite well enough to go sledding," DeVaux reminded her gently.

"I'm going down now." The boy squirmed out of her grasp and threw himself onto the sled. Caldwell watched Lady Whitcombe draw a sharp breath and hold it tightly until her son was safely at the bottom. He plopped gently over at the end of the run, then lay there, helpless as a beetle on his back.

"Oh dear," she murmured. Caldwell thought the faintest ghost of a giggle might have come from her throat, but she stifled it.

The three of them watched as several of the other children attempted to hoist the boy to his feet. The procedure was not going well.

"I'll go to him," DeVaux said with an impatient sigh.

Caldwell remained beside the woman, silent, refusing to make toady small talk, bow and scrape, or just take himself off like a good little nobody.

Nothing passed between them for a long moment. Then, obviously discomfited, Lady Whitcombe clasped her gloved hands and shot him a tentative smile. "Jordan thinks I coddle the boy too much," she said.

"Perhaps you do," he replied brusquely. He knew if she had been a plain, unpretentious country girl he would have treated her very differently. But something about her London manners, not to mention the grand pretension of her title, set his back up.

She looked slightly taken aback, but he had to give her credit for poise. "Perhaps so." Her pleasant but uninviting smile fixed to her face, she turned away to look for DeVaux, the conversation closed. He had thought her attractive when she was talking to her son, but now her face was blankly inexpressive. Still beautiful, but not in the least bit interesting.

"He seems like a fine child," Caldwell said gruffly at last.

"He's not very well. I worry about his catching a chill."

She evidently was the shabby genteel sort: title, but no money. And he could see from the way she was twisting her gloves that she was quite uncomfortable with him. Frightened almost. He resisted the urge to say something outrageous just to watch her flutter.

He wondered idly what her husband was like. A bluff, jolly lord, unable to deny himself his port and beef despite the fact that the bills went unpaid? No, a woman with her looks would have married someone dashing. A handsome spendthrift. A Bond Street beau. Someone who fit the aristocratic notion of romantic.

A title and a love match. Besides blunt, who could ask for more? A healthy child perhaps, but it didn't look to him as if there was anything wrong with William that a little less mother smothering wouldn't cure.

DeVaux and William were coming up the hill. The boy, now divested of one scarf and an entire coating of wool, was smiling happily and chattering to the professor. DeVaux cheerfully waved the

clothing at Lady Whitcombe, as though counter-
manding her dress code stipulation was entirely
within his rights. John saw the woman's lips thin.

He felt a renewed surge of dislike. There was
something about her that aroused a part of him
that he didn't really care to acknowledge. Her reserved poise left him feeling a bit gauche,
underbred.

He pushed away such unrepublican notions, but
still resented her for evoking them. Lord and Lady
Whitcombe and their cozy life. He wondered, ir-
relevantly, if her husband appreciated her cool
beauty or if he had a mistress or two on the side like
most men of the *beau monde.*

"What does your husband say?" The words
popped out before he could stop them. "About
William's health, I mean."

Lady Whitcombe waved at her son and smiled.
Then she drew herself up and looked at him with a
glance colder than the February day. "My husband
is dead."

"Forgive me," he said with a slight bow. He felt a
stab of guilt. No husband. No pretty life. And most
assuredly none of his business.

She said nothing, but turned to welcome
William.

"I feel better," the boy said, panting a little from
his climb up the hill. "I'm not so hot." He took his
sled from DeVaux and settled himself on it with the
same intent determination John had seen on his
mother's face. "I'm going again. And this time,
don't come help me. I'm not a baby."

The woman watched him go, then turned to De-
Vaux. "Jordan, tell him—"

"Eleanor," his friend said in a warning tone.
"He's fine."

Lady Whitcombe looked as though she would very much like to throw herself down the hill after her son, but instead merely ran to the edge of the ridge, watching anxiously and calling out sharp warnings at frequent intervals.

"Why are you wearing such a hangdog expression?" DeVaux demanded, looking Caldwell over as though for the first time.

"Cold," he replied, noting with dissatisfaction that the syllable hung in the air in a white cloud. Then he grinned. "But I'm not leaving before I get a ride in the bathtub."

DeVaux laughed and watched as the trio of students tumbled into the snow, arms and legs windmilling madly. "Might have a go myself."

"So how do you know her ladyship?" Caldwell asked, jerking his chin toward where Lady Whitcombe was standing with her gloves pressed to her mouth in fear.

DeVaux shot him a smirk. "There's no need to get your back up." At John's look of surprise, he laughed all the harder. "You only put on the Cheapside accent when you feel threatened. She's not like the rest of the gentry. So there's no need to bring out the guillotine, Citizen Caldwell."

Caldwell could not help but laugh too. "Am I so predictable? And so prejudiced? I promise I shall behave the perfect lamb. With a very educated accent. After all, I have gotten over your inheriting a title. Which was quite magnanimous of me, considering you were already a pompous windbag."

"I don't know how you managed. I really don't," DeVaux replied mildly. "But I know you'll be good enough to forgive Lady Whitcombe her lamentable breeding as well. After all, she is an old family friend. She lives a very retired existence just down the road, in Potton. A life so modest even you would approve of it. I thought it would do some good for her and the boy if they were to get out and about a bit."

"Not from London?" he asked in surprise, though of course he hadn't meant to show any interest at all. He watched a moment to be sure William could right himself on his own. The boy did so, after a minimum of flailing, and began doggedly trekking up the hill again.

"Oh yes, she used to live in London," DeVaux went on. "But I believe she came to hate the place as much as you do. She rarely leaves Potton. I bribed her here with an offer to ask Dr. Stalk to see William, but in truth, I wanted to see the boy get out a bit more. She coddles him."

William had come up the hill. John could see that he was wheezing slightly. Lady Whitcombe crouched in the snow and examined him with concern. He felt an uncomfortable twinge of sympathy. "I suppose he's her only family."

"He is," DeVaux said. "But he'd benefit a sight more from the society of boys his age and a bit more fun. Too serious, that boy."

"I often say the same about you," Caldwell reminded him. "Haven't been able to drag you out for a pint in a week."

DeVaux grinned. "True. But today I will remedy that. We are having luncheon at the Three Tuns, and I have hired a sleigh to take Lady Whitcombe and her son home. Will you join us?"

Spending the afternoon in the company of a serious little boy whose cold, proper mother brought out all his East London insecurities was really not his idea of a good time.

"Gladly," he heard himself say.

"Excellent." DeVaux looked well pleased. He crossed his arms across his chest in a gesture that suggested it was all settled.

They watched as Lady Whitcombe reluctantly let William set off on another run.

"Widowed," Caldwell muttered. Perhaps that was why she looked so sad. He looked up to find that DeVaux was shaking his head. "No, no," he protested, alarmed. "I shall not step on your toes." Lord knew, she was a world away from the kind of woman he would pursue.

"It isn't that. I have no designs on her myself, I assure you." DeVaux looked grave. "It's just that, well—"

"Above my touch, eh?" he said with a roll of his eyes.

"No," DeVaux said thoughtfully. "It isn't that. It's just that, well, her first marriage wasn't particularly happy. I doubt she is very interested in a second one."

He shrugged. He himself wasn't particularly interested in a first one.

"And don't," DeVaux said, sticking a finger into John's face with unexpected venom, "think that you can make her an offer less than marriage. I swear I'd kill you."

Caldwell held up his hands in a gesture of placation. "It hadn't crossed my mind." Virtuous, well-born widows with sickly children were hardly his style.

"She isn't that kind of woman."

"Of course she isn't," he said in surprise. "She's a lady." One didn't have to be raised in Mayfair to know the rules. Ladies did not consort with the lower orders. They lived out their dull, proper lives drinking tea, spending money, changing clothes, and presenting their husbands with occasional children. He looked at his friend, but DeVaux seemed to have calmed already, the red flush dying down from his cheeks.

"Yes," the professor drew a breath. "A lady. And don't forget it."

Caldwell gave him a thin smile, then glanced at the elegant woman standing in the snow. "I'm hardly likely to."

Chapter Two

William was not eating enough. Oh, he was pushing the slice of ham around on his plate, but he was primarily engaged in his intent conversation with Jordan's friend Professor Caldwell.

Eleanor caught her son's eye and gestured to his plate. He obediently lifted a forkful of carrot, but it was arrested halfway to his mouth when Caldwell began to demonstrate some principle, energetically diagramming something with a pencil on a scrap of paper.

She saw DeVaux watching her and turned her attention back to her own meal.

"He's fine, Eleanor," DeVaux murmured.

She nodded brightly and asked him some question about his research. Jordan was a gem, and of course she owed him everything, but there was no way he could understand. Perhaps there was no way anyone could understand.

She shook herself and forced a smile and nod to DeVaux's response. She was just being overly dramatic, worrying so much over Will's health. Her husband had often enough accused her of that.

And it didn't help that she was feeling a bit self-conscious, out in public for the first time in so long. Perhaps she was only being fanciful in thinking everyone was watching her, knowing everything. Jordan's friend not the least.

The man was affable, and certainly seemed to be cheerfully putting up with William's unending stream of questions. But there was something almost impudent in the way he looked at her that made the hairs rise at the back of her neck. It was as though he was really looking into her, assessing her.

As though he could see into her past.

She resolved to avoid his company in the future. She looked up and found those penetrating eyes upon her again.

She didn't like him. Not at all. He was too handsome, too clever. He had a deceptively boyish look, his russet hair too long and falling into his frank hazel eyes. But his laughing expression stilled when he looked at her, and the hard expression around that well-formed mouth made him look almost dangerous.

She suppressed a shudder and turned to DeVaux, full in the swing of a humorous story of the exploits in his college: the students' misadventures and deep contrition, and his own colorful ways of devising punishments to fit their crimes.

"You will be an excellent father someday," she said, laughing.

He put his hand to his heart as though she'd stabbed him. "Perish the thought. Never. I'm a confirmed bachelor."

She watched him closely for a sign of regret. After all, long ago, when she was in the midst of her own terrible upheaval, he too had suffered a heartbreak. Did she herself appear as recovered as he did?

"Don't you think you would be more comfortable with a wife?" she could not help asking.

"Comfortable?" he echoed with a loud laugh. "I should say not. It would make my life a thousand times more inconvenient. Think on it, now I take my meals at the university, have a woman in to clean my chambers, another university maid to darn my socks. . . . All the things a wife could do to make my life more comfortable are already done by Mother Trinity. Do you not agree, Caldwell?"

Caldwell, who appeared to be deeply involved in sketching out elaborate greenhouse plans with William, looked up. "Not entirely," he said with a grin.

Eleanor was surprised that he had been following their conversation. "See?" she said to DeVaux. "Your friend agrees with me. A wife would provide you with companionship." She had the distinct feeling that Caldwell might have been referring to companionship at its basest level, but still, the point was perhaps the same.

"And Mother Trinity shares her favors with a great deal too many others," Caldwell added, his droll, calm delivery at odds with the laugh that lurked just behind his voice.

Such a cynical man. And critical as well, if his slightly bored expression was any indication.

DeVaux rolled his eyes. "Nonsense. A wife is a wife. The details would be different, but the primary decision would be whether to have one or not. And I decided long ago that I would prefer to be boiled in oil before I would take a wife."

"I never knew you to be such a misogynist," she protested with a laugh.

DeVaux looked wounded. "Indeed, I am not. It is marriage I am opposed to, not women. To be in the constant company of the same person for the rest of my life? Man or woman, I find the idea horrify-ing. And to be honest, madam, I'm surprised to hear you defending the institution."

Eleanor felt herself blushing hotly. How provoking of Jordan to bring up her past in front of a stranger. Especially one whose eyes seemed to miss so little. To her surprise, the professor did not ask for an explanation. Instead he merely handed his pencil over to William and then leaned lazily over the table.

"You are imagining marriage untenable because you are imagining the wrong person," Caldwell said after a long moment. He had a peculiar way of smiling in which only the corners of his mouth turned up. It made him look sarcastic, as though he was laughing at them all.

"And what, sir, would make the right woman?" she asked. She was sorry she had asked it. It was the kind of question that at a London ball might have been deemed arch. She had even heard the echo of her old flirtatious voice in the comment. Good Lord, but old habits died hard deaths. Put her in the company of a few bachelors, and she was preening and carrying on like a girl at her first dinner party.

"A woman of character," Caldwell said promptly, as though he'd actually given the topic some prior thought. "A woman of no pretension; of good republican notions of liberty, equality, and fraternity; well-educated; principled; industrious; moral; pleasant company; and a good manager of the household."

"Is that all?" DeVaux asked dryly.

Caldwell grinned. "Perhaps if she was musical, that would be pleasant."

"She sounds deadly dull to me."

"Not at all," he replied with a shrug. "Someone

mild, with an even temperament, would be much easier to live with over the years than someone who was extremely witty or weepy or beautiful or passionate. Any extreme, no matter how alluring at first, would grate on one after some time."

"So you are merely looking for a perfect paragon of womanhood who has no personality whatsoever," Eleanor said with a bit of sarcasm of her own. "I feel certain you can find that. But indeed, what would you offer?"

She wished she hadn't said it. It sounded rude. And more than that, this was a ridiculous conversation. She had no interest in what the man thought of marriage or who would be the ideal mate.

"Me?" There was that curl in his mouth again. "I can offer nothing. No virtue, no money, certainly no title. A bit of education, nothing of modesty, and as for pleasant temperament, the less said the better." He and Jordan roared with laughter together.

"You are musical," DeVaux protested. "Berwild says he can hardly sleep at night with you sawing away melancholy tunes on the violin."

"Ah, well, I see that as more of a tool to annoy my fellow men. You see, Lady Whitcombe, alas I am not husband material. DeVaux here is. He's got the blunt, the style, the title. But as he will not marry, and I cannot marry, I'm afraid we are both doomed to remain bachelors."

"For the best," said DeVaux, "if you intend to marry a woman so despicably full of virtue. I should be obliged to drop your acquaintance immediately."

"Oh, I shall find someone absolutely scandalously full of virtue," Caldwell retorted. "Someone like Lady Whitcombe here." That horrid crooked smile again. "Only, of course, a great deal more dim-witted. To ensure she'll accept me, of course."

She looked sharply at DeVaux's friend, a sudden panic squeezing her corset. Had Jordan divulged her secret? No, of course not. It was only idle talk.

"Nonsense," she said weakly.

She looked down at the gravy congealing on her plate, determined not to let Jordan catch her eye. He knew of her past. It was anything but virtuous. He of course never judged her for it. But if his critical friend knew. . . .

The man's eyes were too sharp. He would see in a second that there was some secret to be exposed, and she knew by the twist of his lips that he would find the virtuous veneer over her black past deliciously humorous.

"Professor Caldwell," William said, emerging from the heavy fog of his own ruminations. "I am worried that there isn't enough room for the melons in the greenhouse. I just don't see how it can be done."

She felt Caldwell give her one last searching look, and then he turned back to answer her son.

For the rest of the afternoon, as the early evening yawned quickly over the blue-white landscape, Eleanor concentrated on disappearing.

She was adept at it, really. She had learned in the last nine years to make herself all but invisible. The townspeople in the little town of Potton would have described her as quiet, private, humorless, perhaps even cold. No one would have recognized in her the mad, laughing, passionate butterfly she had once been. No, no. Wings tattered, she had slunk into the countryside and crept back into her cocoon.

She bit the inside of her cheeks to keep from

laughing when Caldwell answered with outrageous replies to William's constant questions. She pressed her lips together to seal in a pert response to the man's temptingly critical comments on London life. It was difficult, but she had had plenty of practice. Plenty of time to learn to avoid drawing any curious gaze.

But Caldwell, confound the man, was not so easily put off. As they climbed into the sleigh that Jordan had so kindly hired, he turned the same charm he had used to win William's instant hero worship upon herself.

Will had asked to be shown how to drive, so he and DeVaux sat on the box, and there was nothing left but for Eleanor to ride in the back with Caldwell. Apparently the man didn't have a home to go to. If he found her presence so very distasteful, he should take himself off. But of course that wouldn't be half so much fun for him.

She could see by his infuriatingly amused expression that he knew very well that she did not wish for his company.

"It is a beautiful night," he said, innocently enough.

Eleanor looked up. The low snow clouds of the day had cleared and the sky was a clear, vaulted black, shimmering with stars. Now that they had left the town of Cambridge behind, there was no sound but the hiss of the runners on the snow and the jingling of the horses' harnesses. The air was so still, so perfect in its sparkling whiteness, it almost felt wrong to speak. "Indeed," she said, almost whispering, "very beautiful."

She pulled the rugs closer under her chin and wished harder that he hadn't chosen to accompany them.

"How do you know Professor DeVaux?" he asked.

It was an ordinary question. A polite one, only. He likely didn't care what she answered. But she felt herself go tense anyway. "Our families know each other," she replied, repeating the lie they had agreed upon long ago.

The horrid man didn't know when to stop. He cocked his head in the way William did when he was curious. "He was friends with your husband, I suppose?"

She swallowed the bile that rose in her throat. "He knew Whitcombe, yes." There, that was truth enough.

"I'm very sorry for your loss. I'm sure your son is a great comfort to you. He's a very bright boy. His father would be proud."

Her head snapped around to stare at him, but the man's chin was tilted up, his eyes fixed intently as he studied the stars. Eleanor willed her pounding heart to slow. Professor Caldwell was an astronomy professor, like DeVaux. He was thinking about the heavens, only making idle drawing room conversation to make her think he gave a hang about her life.

"I'm certain he would," she responded. Whitcombe had died a year ago, it was true. But she didn't particularly wish to mention that she hadn't seen the man in nearly ten years. After only eight disastrous months of marriage they had kept very separate abodes.

She and Professor Caldwell sat in silence for so long that she began to relax. Perhaps she should ask him a question, steer the conversation away from herself. Something innocent, perhaps about his employment at the university.

But during her time in the country, with no one to talk to but herself, William, and the vegetables in the garden, she seemed to have lost her knack for conversing with ease. "Do you enjoy—"

"May I ask how he died?"

Too late! She mentally rained several colorful curses upon his head. She drew a breath and watched the countryside slide by. It didn't look so beautiful anymore. The jagged shapes of the naked trees poked sharply into the sky. The smooth blanket of snow appeared stifling.

"He died on the Continent. In Belgium."

"Diplomat?"

"Gin."

For the first time, Caldwell turned his face from the sky and looked at her, his straight brows raised slightly in surprise. "I'm sorry," he said at last.

She wasn't, of course, but she could hardly say that. And perhaps she should make it clear that Whitcombe had not been a government man at all. Just a rotter.

Instead she said nothing. All she could hear was the dull pounding of the blood in her ears, the fear shrilling through her nerves. He knew, he knew, he knew. But of course he didn't.

"One must move on," she said at last. "Whitcombe acknowledged William as his heir; we have what little income was left from the estate, and we have a comfortable life in Potton now." She felt slightly disgusted at the pious tone in her own voice.

His face was turned to the sky again. "A comfortable, virtuous life in Potton. I'm afraid I misjudged you. When I first met you, I thought you were some grand, titled London lady, all pretension and hypocrisy. I grew up in London, and I grew to hate all that."

She felt an unexpected wave of regret. She had

been a part of that pretension and hypocrisy. And it had ruined her. "I did too. I found London a very lonely place."

He laughed. "Lonely? I never thought it that. But I imagine we grew up very differently there. In Cheapside one is never lonely."

He said the words as though he expected her to recoil in horror. She shrugged. "I didn't grow up in London. I went there only after my marriage. I enjoyed it at first. But everything about my life there, the friendships, the flirtations, the whole lifestyle, it was all built on nothing."

She probed those memories gently, wondering if they would still hurt. Surprisingly, they didn't. Like the dullness of scar tissue, there was no sensation at all. "I never went to Cheapside," she mused.

"I imagine you wouldn't. Just as I never went to Mayfair." She thought she heard bitterness in his voice, but it was gone when he spoke again. "DeVaux, of course, annoyed me a great deal when I first met him. He forced me to revise my opinion of titled gentlemen. I'd thought them all idlers and wastrels. And then DeVaux had to come along and be such a dashed hard-working, sincere, despicably good person." He shook his head. "Utterly disappointing."

"He can be quite pompous," she said consolingly.

"Yes, thank God." He heaved a sigh. "I do hope you will not force me to revise my ideas of grandly titled London ladies."

She turned her face back up to the sky. "Oh, I didn't turn out at all as I was expected to," she said, far more sincere than he knew.

Chapter Three

Eleanor carefully locked the front door and then paused to tie on her narrow poke bonnet. Better to put it on outside where she couldn't see it than in front of the glass where she was reminded of how very dowdy it was. Ah well, fashion didn't matter here in Potton. And certainly she should be beyond thinking about it.

She recalled with embarrassment how carefully she had dressed herself for the sledding outing yesterday. Still prone to little vanities. Ah well, she'd been well paid back by Jordan's friend's scornful look. Laughably, he seemed to think her as proud as a duchess merely because of her title.

She couldn't help but smile. She had a great many faults, but pride certainly wasn't one of them. That had gone by the wayside long ago.

She set off down the walk with the market basket over her arm. Doing the daily shopping was hardly a peeress's work. She turned and gave William a cheerful wave where he was studying a book by his bedroom window and then turned to tromp down the snowy lane.

She could still see the runner marks from the sleigh. How lovely it had been to go for an outing—despite Professor Caldwell's distressing presence.

And besides his snubs, nothing terrible had happened. No one had gasped and pointed out the notorious Lady Whitcombe. No one had pulled their children away from her contaminating presence. Or their husbands.

Jordan was right. Perhaps she should get out more.

She swung the basket as she walked, enjoying the invigorating snap in the air. Yes, perhaps after all these years, she was finally getting used to her new life. And perhaps despite it all, she really had been able to start over.

Potton was hardly a metropolis, but on market day it drew a fair number of farmers and tradesmen to the small town square. The cobbles were swept clean of snow, and there was a temporary labyrinth of wooden stalls and tables overflowing with beef and cheese, dry goods and tinware. She loved the crowd and push of it. After so much solitude during the week, it was like walking back into real life.

"Fish, madam? I have some lovely salt cod. You won't find better."

"Hot meat pies. Try one now, take half a dozen home for dinner!"

"Shoes mended while you wait. All kinds of leather goods mended!"

Eleanor shook her head and moved toward the stall that stood in the shadow of the Tin Bell inn, where an elderly Yorkshireman sold herbs and remedies.

"Where is William?" asked a voice at her elbow.

Eleanor looked down and saw a pair of boys William occasionally played with. She smiled. "He did not come with me today. We went sledding yesterday, and I am worried he might have caught cold."

The older boy, perhaps Will's age, gave a great roll of his eyes. "He's always sick. Tell him we want him, as we are stockpiling a great many snowballs to lay siege on Mary Martindale and her sisters."

Eleanor was not very impressed with the boy's forward manners, but she nodded gravely. "I'm certain he will be better tomorrow."

The younger boy, a duplicate of his brother but with a shock of red hair instead of blond, looked up from where he was examining a scab through the hole in his trouser knee. "Are you a Moor?" he asked suddenly.

"I'm sorry?" She looked down at him. "I'm not sure what you mean."

The boy was temporarily distracted by the squealing courtship taking place between a very pretty girl minding a stall full of ribbons and trimmings and a young buck recently disgorged from the Tin Bell.

"A pair of Moors," repeated his brother. He gave the red-headed boy a hard elbow, then turned insolently back to Eleanor. "Pa says that Will is a bastard because you and someone were a pair of Moors."

"Paramour," she corrected, pretending she could not feel the hot blush creeping up her cheeks. "Tell your father it isn't his concern."

The boys looked at each other, wiggling with pleasure over their own boldness. "I know what a bastard is," the younger volunteered.

"Run along, boys," she said in her most severe tone. She wasn't sure they understood the subtlety of a coldly arched brow. Their parents, she knew, were more prone to the shouting and ear boxing approach to discipline. But nonetheless, they evidently thought she might be capable of that tactic as well, for they fled, giggling.

Eleanor turned back to the stall, determined to remain outwardly unperturbed. She took a deep breath, focusing on the rich smells of the dried thyme, verbena, and mallow root hanging in bunches across the top of the stall.

There was no point in getting upset.

She was picking out several tinctures that the Yorkshireman assured her were good for inflammation of the lungs when she felt a presence very close behind her. She turned, half expecting the horrid little boys again.

"Sorry, madam," said the young man from the Tin Bell. "But I couldn't help but notice you." He gave her a cheeky grin, a bit the worse for the sprouting of stubble around it.

As anyone would agree that this was not the appropriate mode of introduction, she merely gave him a disapproving look and went back to sifting some coriander seeds through her fingers.

"You're the widow Lady Whitcombe," he went on, oblivious to her cut. "My country estate is not far from here. Just here for the month, you know. Rusticating a bit, I'm afraid. You know how the demmed duns get. I thought I needed a spell in the outerlands. Fancied it would be quite dull, but perhaps I was wrong. I thought I'd heard you lived hereabouts."

Eleanor cast a glance at the ribbon girl who had been the previous focus of the man's attention, but she was now carrying on a shrill flirtation with the cheeseman's son.

"Excuse me, please," she said, turning to go. She would get her tinctures later. At the moment, it was more important to extricate herself from this.

"Tillard," the man called out to a nattily dressed companion just reeling out of the Tin Bell. "I've just come across Lady Whitcombe."

The two fell in step beside her as though they were all the best of friends. The sour, smoky smell of the taproom was strong off them both.

"You recall Lady Whitcombe," the first man said, giving his friend an elbow in his fashionably nipped-in waist. "A high flier in London, one of Arthur DeVaux's set."

Eleanor quickened her pace, striding toward the stall that sold tin pots and kettles, half thinking she would brain them with one if they kept this up.

Arthur DeVaux. Jordan DeVaux's cousin. It had been a long time since she'd allowed herself to think of that name. He'd been the ringleader of a rather wild group of the wealthiest, most fashionable and most dissolute members of the ton—the very opposite of his serious, academic cousin. Arthur and his cronies had been hard drinkers, light dancers, mad gamblers, and relentless spenders. The London years she'd spent in that set had been a frenzied blur of hedonism. She shuddered.

"I must ask you to leave me," she said, turning on the men when they showed no signs of abandoning her side. "We have not been introduced, and this is not proper conduct."

They looked at her for a moment in rather dull-witted surprise. "Didn't think you'd care about proper conduct," said the stubbly one. "Heard you were right good fun. And Arthur's crowd knew right good fun." Oblivious to her discomfort, they followed her as she walked quickly on again. "He lived the way men should live: go in for pleasure; go out in a duel; never pay the tradesmen's bills." He gave a loud horsey laugh. "It's the way I want to go. Too bad about the duel though."

"I haven't lived in London in many years," she said coldly. "I live very quietly now, and I ask only to be left alone."

The men loped along behind her, batting at ribbons and sausages in the stalls as they passed. "True, true," said Tillard. "It's been a long time since the days you were there, eh? Were you still around when Hayhurst set his hair afire? No, don't suppose you were. Too bad you left, you know. Mimi Browning still has her weekly soirées. What a laugh they are. Quinn blew his brains out, you know. Lost everything overnight. Hazard, of course. Pity. Did Whitcombe send you off to this backwater?"

Good Lord, this was worse than she'd imagined it would be. Farmers withdrew behind their cabbages and looked disapproving. Their wives murmured behind their hands to each other and stared at the tipsy men.

The dandy gave his companion a broad wink. "I mean, the word was that there was a *reason* for your going. And it wasn't Whitcombe's reason, if you take my meaning."

She was panicking, walking faster and faster through the maze of stalls. There must be a way to be rid of them. But everywhere she turned in the market, they followed, jovial, stupid, drunken.

"Is that so, madam? No need to be shy about it. We're not provincial rubes like . . . like these people." He waved his hand to encompass the marketplace.

"I'm going to the constable," she announced.

"Ah now, don't fly up into the boughs," the first man insisted, linking his arm with hers. "We mean no harm. Just wanted to get the story straight. Kind of thing happens all the time. And Whitcombe acknowledged the sprig, if I recall."

Lord, where was the constable when one needed him? In another moment she would give up on not making a scene and would grab the idiots by the hair and knock their heads together.

She was dashing along at a very undignified pace, but the wretches kept up, cheerfully oblivious. "You should come back up to London," Tillard mused. He picked up an apple from a stand and took a loud bite. "Much better fun than this backwater," he informed the indignant grocer. "After all, you're a merry widow, right? Better reason than ever. Town needs more company like you. Cut quite a dash in your day. And you haven't lost your looks, I must say."

"Fine-looking specimen," his friend put in.

"Fine-looking specimen," Tillard agreed. "Haven't seen such a prime piece in this age."

"Should come up to London," said the stubbly one.

"You're wasted here," the dandy said scornfully. He made a great show of taking a pinch of snuff and sneezing daintily into his handkerchief. "Now, fair widow, now that we have rediscovered you, you must allow us to buy you a drink at the Bell. Very dry air, in the winter. And powerful cold. You must warm up. We have a private parlor, you know. And of course, considering our mutual acquaintances, we're practically old friends."

"Sir." She nearly ran the last few steps toward the constable and took his arm. "I must beg you to make these men leave me. I do not know them, and they will not leave me alone." Heavens, in another moment she would disgrace herself by bursting into tears of frustration and humiliation.

The two men looked rather affronted, and at the constable's scowl ambled off in the direction of the Tin Bell.

"Thank you," she said. She could feel her legs shaking and the sweat starting out along her scalp. She should be used to it. There was a time when these kinds of things happened all the time. She should handle them with coolness and grace, or at least with calmness, after all this time. And at least this time Will was not here.

But it had been a long time since people had confronted her so directly. She'd thought that after all this time the gossip had been reduced to a smattering of odd stares and comments behind the hand.

The constable was looking down at her with the same scowl he'd used on the town bucks.

"Thank you," she repeated, releasing his arm. "Your intervention was very timely."

The man tugged his waistcoat over his blooming girth as though she had rumpled him. "We have enough difficulties on market day without ladies drawing trouble on themselves by talking to drunken popinjays." He gestured toward where two girls in a stand full of turnips were calling and waving to a crowd of young men. "Then they come running to me for help, trying to preserve some fiction of maidenly modesty. All for show."

She felt a surge of fury that threatened to overcome her relief. No, this was not the time to attempt an explanation. Unable to look the constable in the face, she thanked his waistcoat, bobbed a quick curtsey and walked—no, nearly ran—back toward the red and yellow sausage-roll tent that marked the way to the lane home.

Jenny, their maid of all work, would have to do the marketing later. She couldn't finish it today. Not when those men, or others like them, might be hanging about, ready to pounce on her with their bluff, drunken humor and their too-sharp memories.

At last she was out in the countryside again, panting with the speed of her gait, the basket banging awkward and empty against her hip.

Very well. It was over. And it was nothing worse than a bit of embarrassment. At least they hadn't propositioned her, as they sometimes did.

Sticks and stones. Sticks and stones.

She could see the place in the snow where De-Vaux had turned the sleigh around and headed back to Cambridge. Faithful Jordan. Her only friend through it all. It was thanks to Arthur's cousin that she hadn't had to suffer more humiliation in London. At least here in Potton, most people left her to her own devices.

She wondered, merely to distract herself, how long it would be before Jordan's friend Professor Caldwell found out her whole story. That was, of course, presuming he cared enough to ask about it. With his bourgeois morality heightened by the snobbery learned in the ivory tower of Cambridge academics, he would likely laugh that scornful smirk right off his face when he found out that a prime example of the immoral ton lived among them.

Ah yes, he would doubtless feel quite vindicated to hear that this grand London lady had just as blemished a past as he could wish.

Chapter Four

Potton was on the way to nowhere. Or at least nowhere John cared to go. It was nothing more than a rutted road and a cluster of picturesquely run-down cottages slumped in the bottom of a dell. There were hundreds of other towns just like it. This one, perhaps, having the distinguishing characteristic of being the most forgettable.

He dismounted his horse in front of the tidy whitewashed cottage that sat on the edge of the town, wishing again that he had some brains in his head. But no. He'd awakened this morning with the crackbrained idea that today would be a lovely day to ride out to Potton, and his body had readily complied before his forebrain had a moment to object.

Oh well, he needed to get out of Cambridge for the day. He'd had another quarrel with the Master, this time about the fact that he had had the temerity to play his violin on a mild Sunday afternoon. The way the man carried on, you'd have thought he was scraping away at some vulgar sailor's drinking song instead of a quiet minuet.

It was always something. He needed to clear his mind of the repressive, staid air of that place.

And since he was in Potton, he might as well visit

the widowed Lady Whitcombe and her son. His forebrain made a muffled noise of derision, but he ignored it.

As he looked up at the cottage, the objections in his head grew louder. Was it possible that the man at the inn had given him misinformation? The cottage in front of him did not look like the kind of place he'd pictured for the elegant Lady Whitcombe.

It was clean and neat, to be sure, but even the bright coat of whitewash and carefully trimmed hedges couldn't disguise the fact that the cottage was old and small, and had a roof that sagged slightly under the weight of the snow that covered it.

He smiled. Again, he was forced to revise his opinion of grand London ladies, and of her in particular.

He ignored the strong feeling of foolishness that crept over him and strode up the tidily swept walk.

He hadn't expected that she herself would answer his knock. He'd assumed there would be a servant. Some country girl, easily impressed by his second-rate top boots and only passably cut coat. A naïve maid wouldn't think to question his flimsy— well, frankly, rather nonexistent—reason for being here.

But instead Lady Whitcombe herself stood in front of him, her gray eyes paralyzing him, her brows arched higher on her white forehead in an expression of slightly arrogant curiosity.

"You," she said.

Oh, excellent. She sounded as though men like him should come knocking at the tradesmen's entrance. Very well, he could play at that game.

"Lady Whitcombe," he said in his best Cheapside

accent, executing a bow that was more like a pull of the forelock. "A fine morning to ye."

She looked surprised, and then a bit cross. "Will you come in?" she said at last, recovering her manners.

Her hair was a rich chestnut, streaked with fiery reds and golds. It took him by surprise. Somehow such boldly sensual hair seemed out of place on such a reserved cold creature. She evidently agreed, since she'd hidden as much of it as possible under a decidedly dowdy cap.

He followed her into the simple drawing room and allowed her to awkwardly take his coat. Despite the ordinary surroundings there was no doubt that she was a lady. She walked with that affected, graceful carriage that made her appear even taller and more slender than she perhaps actually was. He felt almost hulking in her presence.

"I was in the neighborhood," he said, brutally abusing his consonants. "And I thought I would call."

Her face was placid, but he could see her eyes move restlessly toward the bell pull, the doorway, the window. Beneath that proud expression was something surprisingly like fear.

"I'm sorry to seem ungracious," she said, a faint flush rising up those high cheekbones. "I've had a rather difficult morning at the market, and it has put me out of temper. How kind of you to call. We so rarely have visitors."

It was rather amusing to see her squirm, but she handled his unexpected presence with aplomb. He sat in silence and let her struggle to fill the room with a genteel monologue.

Good God, why was he being so cruel to her? It was unfeeling to make her pay for his own stupidity in coming here. If he was to be quite frank, he was here only because he was curious to see her again. Because despite her proud breeding, he found her intriguing.

He would ask after her health; she would ask after his. Perhaps they would discuss the weather. Then they would flounder for a few moments while he gulped the rest of his tea, and he would take his leave. Intriguing be damned, he should always listen to reason.

"Did your son catch that cold you predicted?" he asked, resignedly launching into the health portion of the program.

Unexpectedly, she smiled. It was not a warm smile, or even an open one, but he realized it was the first time he had seen her lips part in an expression of pleasure. "No. He did not. You will be pleased to know that Jordan was correct. I am a mollycoddling creature who will spoil her child with a surfeit of concern."

She looked slightly more human when she was embarrassed. "It's DeVaux's fault, you know," he said sympathetically. "He's always correct."

"I know." She made a wry face. "And as predicted, the outing has even seemed to have done Will some good. Though of course I do worry that he'll take it into his head to build a dangerous contraption like the one your students made."

He leaned back in his chair. Upon closer examination, it was a rather comfortable house. Rather shabby than grand, really. The ceilings were a bit water-stained, and the chimney in here smoked abominably, but it was cozy besides all that. "Assure him that they did not manage to break their necks. That unappealing fact will dissuade him, I'd imagine."

Caldwell was a little disgusted to find that he was putting an effort into the conversation to seem amusing, to make her relax. And yet she still looked like a deer cornered by a huntsman.

"William will be so pleased you've called," she said as soon as the conversation lapsed for a fraction of a second too long. "He has talked of you ever since you met. He is determined now that we shall have a greenhouse."

"Clever boy," he said. "We'll have him at Cambridge soon, I'd expect."

Did she have any beaux? She wasn't long a widow. Less than a year, DeVaux had said. Though she'd lived in Potton longer, he gathered. Still, it wouldn't be very long before someone began courting her. Likely some titled popinjay who actually admired the cool tilt of her brows and the bland nothings she produced in such a low, cultured voice.

She shifted restlessly again. "If you will wait a moment, I will go and get him."

She was hiding something. The notion struck him even more strongly than yesterday. Surprising that someone so regally dull would have something to hide. He wondered if DeVaux knew. She seemed more frightened than conniving, but still, it would not do if she had designs on him.

He could see her anxiety in the slight tremble in her fingers as she held back her skirts to be certain they didn't accidentally brush against him. Her eyes held his gaze too long, then slid away, alarmed.

Peculiar woman. He wondered again exactly how DeVaux knew her.

She was back in a few minutes, with William in front of her like a shield. The boy grinned, but remembered his manners and came over and bowed.

So preternaturally polite, William Whitcombe. At Will's age, John himself had been a complete ruffian.

"I'll just see to the tea," Lady Whitcombe said softly, as though she hoped no one would notice her presence or absence.

"How are you, William?" he asked when she was gone.

"Very well, thank you. Mama was worried I would catch a chill after our sledding expedition, but I did not."

He wished the boy would sit down. He looked like a stiff little tin soldier standing there responding to questions as though he were being examined.

"Good," he replied. "And what have you been doing since?"

William sighed a worldly sigh and clambered into the seat John gestured to. "Well, since it is winter, I can't start on my greenhouse. But I am making plans for it. This time next year we could have oranges!"

Caldwell didn't wish to disillusion the boy as to the length of time required for fruit trees to grow. "Likely not oranges, but you might have melons next summer." Perhaps the library at Trinity had some stray books on horticulture.

"I wanted oranges. Mama likes oranges. When she lived in London, she had oranges every day."

Of course she did. Oranges and chocolate and beaux and ball gowns. Everything a society lady required.

"Well, she may just have to import them from Seville for a little longer. I'm certain she'll survive." He rose to his feet and wandered the room to examine the rather decent watercolors on the walls.

Likely done by her ladyship's own lovely hands. He wondered if she had any skills that were actually useful.

"How long have you lived here?" he asked. What was taking Lady Whitcombe so long? Had she been so overwhelmed by cowardice that she could not bear to come back into the room?

"All my life."

"Never in London?"

William lifted his shoulders. "No."

John squinted at the boy, bemused. Of course, many London ladies preferred to send their progeny to the countryside to be raised. But he'd never heard of their mothers banishing themselves as well.

Perhaps Lady Whitcombe genuinely hadn't liked London, just as she'd claimed. After all, DeVaux too had said she had not cared for life there. Grand chance of that. All society ladies he knew liked London. Where else could one obtain the necessary fashion fripperies, conveniences, and indulgences required for wasting one's time in a genteel manner?

Perhaps Lord Whitcombe had sent her away. Though he couldn't imagine any husband wishing to be apart from such an undeniably attractive wife. Impossible. And besides, the man was dead now, and she could live wherever she liked.

"Did your father live here?" He felt a flash of guilt. He was asking questions he would not ask an adult. He was committing the unforgivable sin of nosiness.

To his surprise, William considered this for a moment. "My real father?" he asked.

John was taken aback. Real father? As opposed to what? A stepfather? He had assumed Lady Whitcombe had been married only once. Could Will be illegitimate?

"Yes," he said, because he didn't know how to ask what he wanted to know.

So perhaps this was the naughty secret of the virtuous widow. He was surprised to find that he was not as elated as he had expected to be to find this chink in her moral armor.

"No. He never lived here." William didn't seem interested in continuing the conversation. In fact, he seemed slightly bored with the interrogation. "I was thinking we should put it on the south side of the house, where there is the most light, but I'm worried there isn't enough room." He twisted in his chair, squinting toward the back wall.

He had apparently returned to the subject of the greenhouse. "We'll take a look in a moment," Caldwell said. "Does your mother need help with the tea?" Was she making the dashed stuff herself?

"I don't know. Shall we go see?"

The boy slid down from the chair and led the way back toward the kitchen. The hall was dark and narrow, but he could see that William's mother had tried to brighten up the place with colorful prints and a series of jaunty little rugs.

The kitchen was small and old-fashioned. Lady Whitcombe was crouched by the hearth lifting the large iron kettle from the hob. When she saw the two of them she flushed—not the delicate pink of an acknowledged compliment, but the deep red blush of shame.

"I'm sorry to have kept you waiting," she said in a brittle voice. "I'm afraid today is Jenny's day off."

She expertly poured a splash of water into the teapot to warm it, swished it about for a moment, then emptied the water into the slop bucket. Once she'd put the tea leaves into the pot, John stepped over and took the heavy kettle from where she'd rested it on an iron trivet. She stepped back and smoothed her hands awkwardly over the front of her gown.

"There is no need to do that," she said, still sounding cross.

A cloud of steam rose up from the stream of boiling water as he filled the teapot. He could see through the mist that the fine gold hairs around her hairline had gone damp with the heat. If only she'd had respectable, ordinary brown hair.

"Good to know even a titled lady knows how to make tea," he said dryly.

"You insist on believing me to be some pretentious *grand dame*. I assure you I have lived very simply for a long time." Her voice was mild, but he could see he'd put her on the defensive.

"Did your husband prefer the simple life?" What a thing to say. He reminded himself that he didn't give a hang about her or her strangely secret past.

Her smile was stiff and artificial. "My husband and I did not live together in recent years. Do you take sugar? William, run and look in the bread box and see if there are any more scones."

"He must have missed William."

"No," she said calmly. "He did not."

He took a sip of tea and tried to imagine cool Lady Whitcombe amorous enough to have taken a lover. She was undoubtedly desirable. Even he felt it, though she was, of course, not the least in his style. But the chill of so much breeding was hardly conducive to passion.

A voice in his head reminded him that he, like countless others most likely, had come calling on her, panting like a schoolboy.

He put down the teacup with a decisive clank. "I should not have dropped by so unexpectedly," he said with an apologetic shrug. "I've displeased you. I only thought I would call in to you on my way back to Cambridge. Just to tell DeVaux you're both well."

"How kind," she said. "You must tell him that William is in excellent health. I was worried about a slight scratchiness in the throat, but it seems to be quite gone now."

"And you?"

"Me?" She looked at him in surprise, as though it was the last question she expected. "I'm very well."

"You look pale."

Her hand flew to the neckline of her drab gown, and she flushed scarlet once again. She really was a beauty. Perhaps she'd had a lover after all. He should feel satisfied rather than disappointed to find that his impressions of the voluptuously immoral *beau monde* were indeed correct.

"We have scones and a bit of iced cake," William reported from the bread box.

"Grand," he said. "Perhaps we might consider eating here in the kitchen." He should go. Leave her to her quiet, private life while he went back to his treatise and his lecture notes. And then perhaps a pint or two at the Three Tuns and a good flirtation with the barmaid.

"Good." William plopped himself into a chair. "I was just drawing up my plans for a fort when you called. You can tell me the most strategic points for cannon."

John could see by Lady Whitcombe's expression that she would likely prefer that he take a few genteel sips of tea in the drawing room like a civilized guest, collect his hat and coat, and leave.

"Are you a professor like Professor DeVaux?" William asked.

"Yes, we both teach astronomy."

Will chewed his pencil with a look of disappointment. "I don't like maths, and Professor DeVaux says maths are the cornerstone of astronomy."

"But you're very clever in maths," his mother said eagerly. "All your engineering projects are based in maths, you know. We will have to hire a tutor soon. I've taught you everything I know."

Caldwell closed his mouth over an impulsive offer to tutor the boy. He hardly knew her. It wasn't his responsibility to help her or her son out of their difficulties. Besides, with the Master watching his every breath, he could not afford time away for frivolous projects.

The boy rolled his eyes at the subject of tutors and turned back to Caldwell. "Do you live at Trinity like he does?"

"Yes."

"Do you get to use the big telescope at St. John's?"

"Yes." He saw that Lady Whitcombe, pretending to be absorbed in stirring her tea, was listening carefully.

"You must come to visit Cambridge more often," he said to her, watching her reaction with interest. What was her secret? "It will be easy enough for you to find a tutor there for William. But perhaps you have family in the area who would prefer to recommend someone."

"I'm afraid I have no family. And I am not close to my husband's relations." She was on her guard again.

It was like a game. He knew she would be polite. And strangely, he knew she would be honest. Ah, the rules of gentility. He, of course, did not have to play by those rules. "Where did you live before you came to Potton? London?"

"Yes."

"And before that?"

"I was raised by my grandmother, in Surrey." She didn't know how to get out of answering. She wished to be rude so badly, but she couldn't manage it.

He was rather enjoying this. She made a desultory offer of more tea, and he dismayed her by accepting. "Your grandmother? I thought you were married previously."

She shook her head, bemused. No stepfather. So her son was a by-blow. Interesting. He wondered if DeVaux knew the truth of it.

"We go to Cambridge sometimes," Will put in, oblivious to his mother's discomfort and the rising heat of the friction between them. "I intend to go to school there someday. Mama sometimes takes me to a doctor in Cambridge. Dr. Stalk. I don't like him. He has bulgy eyes and he sweats."

"Why Potton?" he asked her.

"Why so many questions?" she countered, a crack appearing in her genteel veneer.

"Just making conversation."

Her smile was so thin it was very nearly a grimace. He nearly laughed out loud. She really was a magnificent specimen.

She toyed with the spoon in the sugar bowl, pressing it so hard he thought she might bend it. "And what of you, Professor Caldwell?" she asked. "What brought you to Cambridge?"

He leaned back with his hands behind his head in a most impolitely relaxed manner. Unlike her, he had nothing to hide. "Me? Well, I left my parents' house in Cheapside and went to work as an apprentice to my uncle, who was a man of business for Lord Haversend. Haversend, though he thought it beneath him to know how many pence are in a guinea, thought I showed some promise and sent me to Eton. Not out of charity, mind you, but with the understanding that I would help out his own son there. Tommy required someone to cheat off of, you see.

He took both the teacup and saucer in his palm like a country farmer and took a long swallow. Let her be shocked to hear his true roots. He'd nothing to hide. "Then, after a stint as an ostler, I spent a year working as an assistant to the astronomer Lord Lane, who then reneged on his promise to recommend me to Oxford.

"I worked with a lens grinder here in Cambridge and was graciously allowed to enroll and attend courses, though of course I wasn't treated as a gentleman student. And then, after a spell as a lowly tutor to a very noble and well-known family of six boys of five different fathers—but who, very like their mother, all had brains the size of a grain of millet—I came back to Cambridge." He leaned back in his chair and drained his teacup. "I'm nothing like a gentleman. And I have no secrets."

William looked up from where he had been scratching his pencil on the paper and muttering to himself about defensive strategies for the fort. "I think it sounds rather grand. I wish I never had to be a gentleman."

If Lady Whitcombe had had a child by a man not her husband, the only way he would be considered a gentleman was if Whitcombe himself had acknowledged him. He wondered if that was the case, but a look at the immobile countenance of the lady in question deterred his questioning.

"What a very colorful past," Lady Whitcombe said coolly. "I see now why you've such a chip on your shoulder. I suppose you feel that your hardships entitle you to judge everyone about you. Your moral strength and determination have won you the right to assume that everyone around you is frivolous and corrupt."

Touché. He deserved that. "I would not presume to judge you, Lady Whitcombe." He raised his brows. "I cannot. You are too full of mystery."

Lady Whitcombe had evidently had enough, and she wasn't about to reveal anything more of herself. "I'm delighted you dropped by, and I do hope you'll tell Jordan that we were well." She drew herself up to her full, elegant height. "Now, if you're done with your tea, may I get your coat?"

And with gracious dexterity and a calm, meaningless smile, Lady Whitcombe very quickly supplied him with his belongings and deposited him outside her door.

Chapter Five

Eleanor sat with her gloved hands clasped tightly in her lap and watched Dr. Stalk examine William.

"Breathe into this," the man ordered gruffly, handing the boy a bladder made of oiled skin. "Take a deep breath and blow the bag up as much as you can with one breath."

Eleanor clenched the folds of her gray cloak and breathed out with the boy. She willed him to push the air out of his lungs, her own breath coming out as long and labored as his. But her lungs held out far longer than his, and she saw that the bag swelled only barely enough to part the sides.

Dr. Stalk scowled and continued muttering to himself. "Don't know why people think they're too good for their own village doctor." He grumbled over his thick shoulder. "I have a great many important patients. I can't be dropping everything to tend to people who show up at my own house in the middle of the night on a whim." He hadn't bothered to light all the candles in his examination room, so he took the bladder over to the lamp and held it in the milky halo of its light.

She hadn't shown up at his house on a whim. It's just that he was the acknowledged best man in the county for respiratory illnesses. He'd always refused to make the trip out to Potton. Unless one was very grand, one came to him. And if one was not very grand, one put up with his grumblings.

So when Will's wheezing and gasping grew worse through the day, and still worse in the evening, she'd had little choice but to bundle him up and take the ten o'clock mail coach to Cambridge.

"I was at a dinner party, you know," Stalk said. "With the Master of Trinity and the Dean of St. John's." He stared at her for a moment to be sure she understood exactly how important he was, his protuberant blue eyes fixed and alarmingly wide. "I don't appreciate being summoned from such a thing for some wheezing child, as though I were nothing but a country surgeon."

She looked around the lavishly appointed room that the doctor used for his consultations. It was a strange amalgam of Louis XIV furniture—sensuous curves and delicate flourishes—and clinical artifacts of his practice. Atop a voluptuously gilded occasional table was a large jar containing what could only be the flayed partial dissection of a human lung. Behind the glossy leather examination couch on which William lay hung a shining range of medical instruments. She repressed a shudder.

"You are well known to be the best doctor for illnesses of the lungs," she said, hoping a bit of flattery would placate the man. "Can you blame me for wanting my son to see the best doctor?" She dragged her eyes away from the rows of scalpels, scissors, and clamps and cast a glance at William. He looked pinched and pale as he drew a noisy breath, so she forced an ingratiating smile for Dr. Stalk.

"Madam, I choose what patients I will take on. I

am in great demand. I do not have to examine every sickly by-blow in the countryside." His wide lips flattened and his brows drew up in a disdainful arc. "Lady Whitcombe, I'm well aware of your past. Though of course"—he drew himself up to his full, barrel-chested height—"I'm too much of a Christian to hold it against you when it comes to treating your innocent son."

He made some notes on a tablet, drawing in his heavy cheeks and sucking noisily on his teeth. "See, I shall write you out a prescription for the apothecary. Give him the tincture twice a day, have him drink strong black tea, and continue the steam baths, of course."

Eleanor pressed her teeth together and squeezed out a smile. "Thank you, sir."

The man cast a look over his shoulder at Will's drooping head. "See, he breathes easier already. He'll be fast asleep in a moment or two." His voice dropped lower. "And then what will we do?"

She started and stared at him. But the expression in those bulging, greedy eyes suggested that he did indeed mean what she thought he meant. She stood, shaking out the folds in her high-necked lavender gown. "I will, of course, pay you your fee."

He approached her until he was so close that she could smell the port on his breath. In fact, the dinner party he had been summoned from had apparently served a fish course, some sort of onion ragout, a beef dish, spinach pie, a great deal of wine and then port on top of it all. His mouth was a veritable archaeological find. She stepped backward, clutching the edges of her cloak to her chest.

"Indeed," he said. "But I was thinking, Lady Whitcombe, that we might come to a better arrangement. I am, as you say, the best respiratory doctor. And your son"—he gestured to the flaccid bag on the table—"does not have healthy lungs, I'm afraid. He will require very careful personal attention on my part if he is expected to recover." His expression wrinkled as though he was thinking quite hard about a perfectly logical business proposition. "And I will require very careful personal attention on your part if I am expected to help him."

"Dr. Stalk," she said repressively. "I have your fee right here. And my widow's portion is quite adequate to cover any fees in the future."

He laid a gentle hand on her arm, oblivious to the fact that she jerked it away and began counting out his fee from her reticule with shaking fingers.

She should have known this would happen. She should be used to it by now.

"Now, now, madam," he said in a reproachful voice, "don't be missish. I'm only offering what might be beneficial to us both. I know a few of your dirty little secrets, so don't act as though you're above accumulating a few more. We could have a tidy understanding. My services for yours. Quite a good bargain for you, I should say."

"Put on your coat, Will; it's time to go home." She looked over to see that her son had fallen asleep entirely. She suppressed the feeling of panic.

"Lady Whitcombe, really, coming here in the middle of the night? What is one to think? Surely you do not wish to waste my time by playing coy. I was given to understand that you are not above this sort of arrangement." He reached out to wrap a thick arm around her waist.

She struggled to unwind it. "Thank you, Dr. Stalk. You relieve my mind about my son. We will leave you now." She slipped away from his grasp and went to wake Will and bundle him into his coat. The little room of horrors was closing in on her. She caught sight of a row of glass jars high on a shelf and tried not to think what gruesome bits of flesh they contained.

Will was breathing a bit easier now, thanks to Dr. Stalk's draught, but the poor boy was exhausted from his efforts. He was far too heavy to carry, so she put an arm around his shoulders and propelled his heavy feet toward the door.

"Don't act so high and mighty, Lady Whitcombe," the doctor said with a look of slightly injured surprise. "After all, a widow with your reputation . . . Well, I can hardly be blamed for—"

She shut the door with a firm click. Her heart was racing. There was no point in being angry, she reminded herself sternly. No point in allowing the hot, furious tears stinging her throat to take over. Dr. Stalk was right. She should hardly be surprised when these things happened. She was, after all, a fallen woman.

"How are you feeling?" she asked Will. "Do you breathe a bit easier?"

"Suppose," he mumbled. "I'm tired. And it's too cold. Must we go all the way back home tonight?"

She wished they didn't. An icy sleet was starting, and they had a long wait at the coaching inn before the mail coach arrived. She considered their finances. She hadn't planned to make this trip tonight. There wasn't enough in her reticule to pay for a room at the inn. She put her arm tighter around Will's shoulders and pulled him along. "We'll manage," she said, more to herself than to him. "You can sleep in the coach."

"Look, Mama," he said, brightening. "There is Professor Caldwell."

Excellent. Just the man she least wanted to see. He had the most annoying habit of turning up when she was in humiliating circumstances. And then prying. Likely he was the one who had been spreading ugly stories about her as well. She'd half a mind to stomp over to him and demand that he keep his nose out of her affairs.

The man crossing the street ahead of them looked a bit like Caldwell, to be sure, but he was partly turned from them, his strides long and purposeful, his head down. On closer inspection she saw that it was indeed her nemesis, despite his uncharacteristic look of intense concentration. His plain greatcoat flapped half buttoned in the cold wind that rattled down the alleyway. If he'd been someone else, she might have felt the motherly urge to tidy him up, button his buttons, retie his scarf.

The man appeared quite deep in thought, not a state she considered natural for the cynical, laughing Professor Caldwell.

However, as though he'd heard Will say his name, he turned and recognized them. She gave a cool nod and wondered if there was any way they could merely say hello and continue on their way. Now, in the middle of the night in a sleet-covered street, was not time to confront him. Particularly when she was still flushed and angry from the doctor's proposition. It was best just to keep her dignity and continue on.

But, curse the man, he came up to them anyway, looking unexpectedly pleased. "Lady Whitcombe, William, you're the last two people I expected to see traipsing about in Cambridge in the middle of a cold, wretched night like tonight."

She pulled her cloak closer. Likely he was pleased

to see her so obviously in a pickle. "I had to take Will to see Dr. Stalk. His lungs . . ."

Caldwell's brows drew together in what looked to be genuine concern. "Indeed. And are you better, Will?"

"A bit better, sir," William replied.

"So late and so far from home," he continued. "It must have been serious indeed. May I escort you where you are going?"

She liked it better when he was being a nosy prude. She didn't trust his expression of worry, the way his handsome face was grave and his voice comforting. He was likely just looking for another way to expose her shame.

"If you like," she said stiffly. "We are going to the Three Tuns tavern to catch the mail back to Potton."

He stopped in the gesture of offering his arm. "The mail? The mail coach doesn't come for hours." He drew out his watch from beneath his greatcoat and shook his head. "You don't want to be hanging about the Three Tuns until then. It isn't a place for ladies and children. Not even at the best of times."

"We will be just fine, Professor Caldwell," she informed him. Standing about in this cold sleet wasn't going to help William any. She pulled the boy closer and began walking toward the tavern.

Caldwell caught up with them in two strides. "I know you cannot go to DeVaux's rooms at Trinity; the porter would not allow you in. They're very sticky there about those kind of things. The Master insists on it, of course. But DeVaux has a sister who lives here in Cambridge. Can you not spend the night at her house?"

Eleanor felt the humiliation rise up her cheeks again. "We have not been introduced," she said.

"One doesn't introduce one's sister to a woman like me." There. It was out. She'd made it clear she knew he was aware of her past and that there was no point in pretending.

He said nothing, his brow furrowed. "Wait." He stopped suddenly in the road in front of St. John's College. "Come this way. It will get you out of this damnable weather."

She was about to protest, but he was wearing that serious, distracted look he had worn when she first saw him crossing the street. His problem-solving expression. He took Will's shoulder and pulled them both along toward the entrance to the college.

She found herself rather unwillingly grateful for his help, but at the same time she didn't like him taking charge of them entirely. She didn't want him to know how helpless and frightened she had felt, standing outside Dr. Stalk's consulting rooms. She didn't want to feel obliged to him.

The sleepy porter at the gatehouse straightened slightly and then recognized Caldwell. He blinked once or twice, registering that there were two other people with him, but Caldwell gave him a cheery wave and the man settled more comfortably back on his chair.

She looked around with sudden distrust. "Where are we going, sir? We're in the middle of St. John's College grounds. I hope you do not have any intention of taking us to your rooms." Surely the man would not be so audacious. She remembered Dr. Stalk, and the bile rose in her throat.

He looked at her with genuine surprise, and then an expression of devilment leapt into his eyes. "How villainous you must think me, Lady Whitcombe. No, I assure you, I am not taking you to my rooms. They are at Trinity. The night porter at St. John's is not quite so particular about these things. Likely because he's so blind he can't tell a woman from a member of the horse guards." He grinned. "I am taking you to the observatory."

Will straightened, suddenly interested. "The observatory? Where you and Professor Lord DeVaux look at the stars? How famous. But we shall not be able to see anything tonight. It's all over clouds."

Caldwell's laugh was unexpectedly warm. Rather pleasant. "Indeed, I'm afraid it's a poor night for star watching," he said. "However, it is warm and private, and you may safely wait there without the least inconvenience while I take care of your travel arrangements." He marched them across the frozen court, deeper into the college.

Eleanor looked around them and suppressed a shudder. She'd grown used to the countryside, perhaps. The tall, gray stone buildings that made up the court seemed so imposing, their windows dark and private. She could see that beyond this court was another one, just as severe. Perhaps it was only the grimness of the weather, but here in the dark, she felt like she'd first felt in London, a country girl far out of her element, about to be ruthlessly judged by the grand institution of Society.

Caldwell surprised her by stopping abruptly at the large stone gateway that separated the first courtyard from the second. He took out a key and pushed it into the small door at the bottom of the gateway itself. It made her think of the Tower of London, or the Bastille.

"I must protest. Professor Caldwell—" She did not feel nervous; she sensed that Caldwell was nothing like Stalk. But she was indignant nonetheless. Likely the man took his doxies here for rendezvous.

That was why the porter hadn't batted an eye. Though, admittedly, it was hard to imagine moral Professor Caldwell doing something so shocking.

"Yes, yes," he interrupted. "You must. And I will ignore you because I'm an overbearing bore. Now, here we are. Up the steps, if you please. Mind the ice. All the way to the top, William."

She stopped at the doorstep and turned around. "I cannot allow you—"

In the light of the lamps hung sparsely around the court, the sleet shone in silvery slashes. Caldwell, at the bottom of the steps, had sparkling ice droplets on his shoulders and sleeves. His overlong hair hung damply into his eyes, making him look positively roguish. She stood for a moment, transfixed.

"In, in," he said with a low laugh. "It's hardly a lair of debauchery, I promise you, Lady Whitcombe."

She didn't wish to be alone with him. Even with William there she was not entirely sure she would not disgrace herself. She would either lose her temper and berate him for his judgmental tale bearing, or she would, God forbid, throw herself into his arms weeping in relief that he had rescued them.

Or worse, she would do something, a turn of the hand, a catch in her voice . . . something that his sharp eyes would not miss, that would reveal how very attractive she found him. She would prove herself the harlot he thought her.

He could feel it even now, she knew. The sexual attraction, struggling inside her like a live thing, wanting to escape. He was recklessly tempting it, standing too close, one arm on the doorframe, his breath held, like hers.

No. She was being silly. She was in control. She

was a lady, born and bred, despite it all. And she had learned a painful lesson about passion's ephemeral nature and the shameful aftertaste it left behind.

"I—"

"I'm not going up, you know," he said mildly, the curl of his lips clearly showing he saw her indecision. "You may make yourself comfortable in the observatory while I go to the Three Tuns and arrange a coach."

Good. He was not coming up. They would not be alone together, so there was no fear she would do anything shameful. She should be glad he was showing sense. "Thank you," she mumbled.

"No need to worry, milady. I know my place," he said with a bow accompanied by a rough laugh.

She lifted her chin. "Professor Caldwell. Let us set things straight between us. I am in no mood for your cross-questioning. And I have no wish to repeat the humiliating farce of our last conversation."

He looked surprised, and to her slight satisfaction, a bit chastened. "I'm certain by now you know my past," she went on. "You know that William is not Whitcombe's child. I live in Potton because I am disgraced. So no more insinuating questions this time if you please."

"Lady Whitcombe, I must—"

She interrupted his stammered apology. "Now, I will thank you to leave off pretending we are not social equals. We are not, but it is because you are an educated, decent, respectable man, and I am a woman with a past."

There was a moment of silence while he digested this. "Thank you," he said after a moment. "For your frankness, I mean." The curl to his mouth suddenly looked more boyish than cruel. "I have judged you for your background, which is the very thing I hate most. My behavior the last time I met you was insupportable. I beg your pardon."

She should have been placated by this graceful apology, but oddly, it discomfited her. She preferred him overbearing and rude. The new, odd look on his face made her feel rather less confident that she would not betray her shameful animal nature. As though the old Eleanor was, perhaps, not quite gone after all.

"Thank you," she said, drawing herself up stiffly.

He looked at her quizzically for a moment, then laughed his mocking laugh. "Devil take it, Lady Whitcombe," he said, shaking his head. "Whatever your past or wherever you come from, you do give a set-down a man could never forget."

Impossible! There was no making sense of him. Very well, she would accept his generosity and fly away with the consequences. As long as he was mocking her, she could keep up enough irritation to ensure that she did not forget herself.

She pulled her cloak closer against the freezing rain that blew through the stone archway, ignored the laughing hazel eyes that dared her to match her wits with his, and turned coolly on her heel to go up the stairs.

Chapter Six

Caldwell trudged back from the Three Tuns. He'd spent a pretty penny bribing the stable hands for a carriage and driver when, on a night like tonight, they could demand nearly any price they set their mind to. And even with the outlay of blunt, the dashed thing wouldn't be ready for over an hour.

Even so, it was better than letting Lady Whitcombe and her son sit in the tavern's common room for the next five hours waiting for the mail coach.

The logical part of his mind reminded him that this wasn't really his concern. And the first person to remind him so would be Lady Whitcombe. She wouldn't take his interference very kindly.

Still, while icy water crept down the neck of his greatcoat and his boots slipped in the muddy street as he made his way back toward St. John's College, he couldn't help but feel altogether somewhat cheerful. It was rather appealing to know that the prim Lady Whitcombe was human. That she could feel frightened and frustrated just like any other mortal.

Though of course he hadn't given her a second

thought, or at least only very rare passing thoughts, since that rather awkward visit weeks ago.

He'd do her a good turn tonight and make sure she got home safely just to show he hadn't meant to offend her. Oh, she'd been mad as blazes that day. And he couldn't really blame her. He'd been abominable.

And now that he knew her secret, he felt worse. An illegitimate son was hardly a crime. But she must think him just as judgmental as the rest of society.

He gave a nod to the porter of St. John's, who was still dozing in his station in the little house beside the gatehouse.

Odd to think of Lady Whitcombe with a lover. She seemed so untouchably proper. Everything about her, from her clothes to her posture, was rigid and uninviting. But despite it all, he had to admit there was something very sensual about her. All the starch in the world couldn't hide it. Or perhaps it was that very coolness that made a man wonder what it would take to warm her to passion.

He needed to find an accommodating tavern maid in the near future if he'd sunk so low as to spend his time considering what it would be like to seduce iron-corseted widows.

He climbed the stairs to the observatory, half wondering if the pair had flown away in his absence. After all, the observatory was hardly the kind of place a lady would want to find herself. Perhaps he should have insisted on waking DeVaux and handing her over to him. He was obviously the only man she trusted.

He regretted for a moment bringing her to the observatory. It was a very personal place for him. Surely, if he'd been thinking, he could have come up with another way to help her without bringing her here.

The stairs opened up into a large square room at the top of the Shrewsbury Gate. His home away from home. It was sparsely furnished—just a few stools and wooden chairs, a modest fire in the grate, and the large telescope in the middle of the room. All around the walls were large windows. On the stone pillars between the windows were star charts and slate boards for making calculations. Tables around the room were littered with tracking and calculating devices.

He was relieved to see that William appeared to have taken seriously his warning not to touch anything. The boy must have been exhausted to resist the lure of so many intriguing instruments. Instead he lay on a wooden bench, fast asleep under his mother's gray woolen cloak.

Lady Whitcombe, her stark lavender gown blending with the shadows, sat upright in one of the chairs beside her son, her hands folded in her lap. She had at least unbent enough to remove her bonnet.

Her remarkable hair was strangely at odds with the rest of her unadorned appearance. It was so rich, so almost wanton in its exotic blend of colors. He pictured it around her shoulders—how long would it be? To her slim shoulder blades? To her waist? It was tightly bound back like the rest of her sensual side, but now he could see, as perhaps her lover had, how tempting it would be to free it.

"I have hired you a coach to take you home," he said with a bow. "They are coming in an hour to fetch you."

She stood, her brows lifted slightly in an aristocratic expression. "You take too much upon yourself, Professor Caldwell. I had already made arrangements to take the mail coach home."

"The mail coach doesn't come until nearly five in the morning. You don't want to wait in the Three Tuns that long. The taproom is rather uncouth this time of night."

He knew she was not pleased with his gesture, but he was surprised by his feeling of annoyance when she shot him a regally condescending look. "You are too kind." She made it sound like an insult. "I see that we have little choice but to accept your arrangements. I will, of course, pay you back for your expense."

"Nonsense." He smiled. "I like to have a woman in distress indebted to me."

Such flattery did not please her; he saw her draw herself up straighter. "I would prefer not to be."

There were many things he did not like about Lady Whitcombe. She was too proud, too cold. But he felt undeniably attracted to her. There was a moment or two, in the sleigh, even at the bottom of the stairs tonight, when he had thought she felt the same fire, but her icy exterior made it impossible to tell for certain.

"I would not have let you take us here if I had known we were to be alone," she said, walking over to the table containing an astrolabe. She reached out a finger to touch it, then resisted the temptation and let her hand drop to her side.

"I brought you here so that you might be more comfortable than at a common inn. No one will ever know you're here."

"It is still not proper." Instead of sounding prim, she sounded a little frightened. He was surprised. He knew she was quite capable of looking down her nose and giving him a sharp set-down guaranteed to quell any rising ardor. Why then was she looking at him as she was now, her pale eyes slightly wide, her mouth tense?

"You know there are no private rooms at the Three Tuns," he continued. "Forgive me if I over-stepped myself. I will wait in the gatehouse until your carriage comes."

"Don't go," she said unexpectedly. "We are the ones who are intruding. You were kind to think of us. Particularly when I know you must have been on your way home to your bed when you came upon us." She did not look so very proud with the shadows softening her face. And her little smile was very nearly warm.

"I was indeed going home to my bed," he said. Lord, even the word conjured up wayward images. He found himself rather wishing she weren't a lady. But then again, what madness might he commit if she were not?

She walked over and put her hands out toward the fire in the grate.

"I am sorry to keep you from it," she said quietly.

He should turn around and go back downstairs to wait in the porter's lodge for her carriage. He should leave her alone. Before he pounced on her like some slavering *roué*.

She turned her back to the fire and looked around the room. The golden light silhouetted her slim figure and gave her alabaster skin a rosy cast that made her look less like a rigid, perfect statue and more like a warm woman of desirable flesh and bone.

"Do you spend much time in the observatory?" she asked.

"Indeed. As you may know, at Trinity we do not have our own observatory. We must use St. John's.

In fact, I was just coming from here when I met you."

"So late?"

"Astronomy must be done at night," he laughed. "And I teach, you know. Tonight we were to have a class on measurement taking. But of course the weather made visibility impossible. Still, I came anyway, as there were a few students who had questions that could best be explained here with the charts."

He walked over to the table and ran a finger over the astrolabe she had just abandoned. "It is frustrating when the weather is foul. Which it is most of the winter. But in summer, we take the telescope out to the roof, and by God, I'd say DeVaux and I spend most of our nights up here."

"I admire your passion for your work," she said in a low voice. She was still by the fire, but he could feel her eyes upon him.

"And I admire your dedication toward your son," he replied. "He's a bright boy." Lord. Laying it on a bit strong. A pretty face and a title and he was toad eating with the best of them.

She smiled, a genuine smile. "He is." Then her face fell. "But his lungs . . . ."

"What did Dr. Stalk say?" he asked, crossing to her. "He is said to be the best physician around, you know. I'm certain if anyone can help William, it's he." Yes, that was it. Talk about her son. Nothing dangerous in that.

"Perhaps," she said in a strange, choked voice.

He looked at her in alarm. "What is wrong? Did he say it is something serious? Stalk is the best, but that doesn't mean he knows everything. You could get another opinion in London, you know. What did he say?"

Her lips tightened. "I don't know." Her face was going very red, and John was surprised to see what looked to be tears standing out in her eyes. "He is not very patient. I don't recall what he said. I was . . . distracted." Her hands were clinging tightly to each other, twisting. "Oh, I don't like that man. He . . . he . . . well, I don't like him."

He hadn't expected this reaction. He couldn't tell if she was angry or about to burst into tears. He urgently hoped it was the former. He didn't like ladies crying. This was far outside his experience. He cleared his throat. "We could find another doctor for William. You shouldn't have to go to someone you don't like."

She turned toward the fire and swiped the back of her hand quickly across her cheeks. Oh God, she really was crying. "I don't need your help," she said in a choked voice. "We can take care of ourselves. We'll be fine. It's just that Stalk is the best . . . and yet . . . and yet, I cannot go back to him. I refuse to see him again."

He looked around for something to give her. A handkerchief? A cup of tea? Smelling salts? Dash it all, what was one to do in a situation like this? "What happened?" he asked helplessly at last.

She drew a shaky breath. For a moment he thought she would not explain, but at last she shrugged. "He propositioned me. I shouldn't be surprised. I should expect it, I suppose, but—" She drew herself up straighter. "I am a fallen woman, it is true. But that doesn't make me common property."

"Of course not." He felt a sudden surge of fury toward Stalk. And a second wave directed at himself. A moment ago, he himself had been lusting after her. No, Lord help him, he still was.

"I beg your pardon," she said, with a gloriously unladylike sniffle. "I didn't mean to become a watering pot."

He put his hand on her shoulder, patting it awkwardly. "Cry away. Dr. Stalk is enough to give anyone the megrims."

She gave a choked laugh. "Oh, don't be kind." She turned and looked up at him, her eyes half baleful. "Be anything but kind."

He was standing too close. And she was far too lovely. His patting hand on her shoulder turned into something more like a caress. "I'm not kind," he said wholeheartedly.

She did not move away, or dash his brains out, or any of the things she should have done. One cool look, one disdainful shudder, and it would have all been right again. Instead she merely stood there, looking so damned . . . vulnerable.

He wasn't certain how it happened, but his arms were suddenly around her. She was much smaller than he'd expected. Tiny-boned, like a bird.

She did not pull away. She only stood there, frozen in fear, surprise, longing—he couldn't tell. He could feel her heartbeat through her gown, so fast it seemed to run together in a hum.

He would stop in a moment and let her slap him. He would release her from his clumsy embrace knowing at least that it had been worth it to feel that she was human, warm-skinned and breathing after all. Her fingers tightened on the sleeve of his coat, but she did not push him away. She made no movement at all, as though she too did not want to break the unexpected moment. He pressed his cheek to her temple, and inhaled the scent of rain in her hair.

This was not happening. This could not happen.

In another moment he would do something inexcusable.

"No." He said the word aloud to make it real.

"No," she echoed, almost inaudibly.

He should not take advantage of her distress. She was not thinking. When she came to her senses she would ring a peal over him that would leave his ears bleeding. She would think him like other men. And even he was not so certain that he wasn't.

"No." She said it more firmly this time. She blinked her lashes as though she were coming back to consciousness.

"Eleanor—"

She stepped back. But her look was not contemptuous, only sad. "I will not be anyone's light skirt. Not Dr. Stalk's, not yours."

"Eleanor—" He must make her understand. "I didn't—"

"I know," she said irritably. "The trouble is not you. It's me." She twitched the collar of her gown higher up her neck and shook out her skirts.

"I was a lady before I became someone's mistress, and I should behave like one. Forgive me. I forgot myself." She wore her cool look again, her full lips tightly compressed.

He straightened his rumpled cravat and smoothed his coat. He could feel the flush of humiliation heating his cheeks. He'd behaved like a panting, pawing greenhorn and been rightly rejected like one. "It is I who should apologize." He crossed his arms over his chest and turned toward the fire. "Dash it all, I seem to do nothing by halves. Too rude, too kind." He gave her a tentative smile. "But for a few moments, between bouts of loathing, we seemed to be getting along rather well."

She pressed her fingers to her mouth and made

a strange noise. He wasn't certain if she was laughing, angry, or perhaps about to blub again. He felt a pinch in his chest and battled the irrational urge to sweep her into his arms once again.

"Will you sit by the fire?" he choked out at last. "I would offer you tea, but we haven't any."

"No, thank you," she said, quite composed again. "I will go and sit with Will."

He flung himself into a chair by the fire and forced a jovial smile. "He is better, I hope?"

"Oh yes, much."

"Excellent."

Silence.

"I hope you'll have DeVaux accompany you if you must see Stalk again."

She sat very straight on the bench beside her son. "Yes. I will."

"Good." And then, after a painful moment. "I hope you will not need to see him. That is, I hope Will is recovered. He does seem much better."

"Yes," she said. "I hope so."

Silence.

He yanked at his cravat. "It must be worrisome for you. With him subject to these attacks, I mean."

She looked at her son. "Yes," she said. "It is. One never knows when they will occur."

"How unfortunate."

"We must hope he improves."

The polite conversation sputtered out between them. He sank back into his chair, defeated. She took her gloves and bonnet into her lap and examined them in minute detail. He pulled one long cognac-colored hair off his sleeve.

They agreed, in stilted tones, that the coach would surely not be very much longer. He lay the hair on the arm of the chair and watched it shine in the firelight.

They agreed that it was much more pleasant to wait indoors than out in the sleet.

And then they merely sat in silence until the lamps began to sputter and the coachman of the hired carriage knocked on the door at last.

Chapter Seven

Caldwell pulled hard at the crowbar and watched with some satisfaction as the curricle's bent fender came slowly back into shape.

Boxty Fuller crouched down beside him. "Grand!" he exclaimed. "Not certain how that happened. After all, I hit the hen coop on the other side."

"And a right good mess you made of it," Mad Jack Kittley piped up. A small flurry of feathers drifted across from his side of the curricle. "You're lucky Mr. Kip didn't kick up a bigger dust about it."

Boxty shrugged, as much as his tight, cornflower-blue jacket would allow. "Kip's a betting man. He understood that my intention was to beat Hillstone *around* the chicken house. Not plow through it. The chickens, of course, were less understanding, but I've paid enough to put everyone to rights." He shoved his hands into the pockets of the canary-yellow trousers meant, Caldwell supposed, to provide an eye-popping foil for the jacket, and gave a resigned sigh. "Now there's just to get the rig back into knick. Good of you to help, Professor. You're dead handy at this sort of thing. Wish we'd had you along when we put together the hip bath sled."

Caldwell made a noise of dismissal. He was handy

at carriage repair for good reason, but he didn't
particularly wish to discuss the stint he had done in
a livery stable during that vague time between re-
jecting his parents' values and settling on his own.
He smiled. Perhaps driving into chicken coops was
Boxty's manner of working through that particular
conundrum of youth.

Conundrum. Like that of Lady Whitcombe. No.
No point in revisiting the events of last week. He'd
made a hash of that for certain. That farce of an encounter should have served as an excellent reminder
that he was cut out for academics, not wooing. Good
God, but he'd wanted her. He felt a renewed wash of
humiliation at the memory of his ham-handed attempt at seduction.

Ah well. She had turned him down with well-bred
firmness, and that was that.

No matter. He'd found in life that pursuing a
willing woman was likely to be far more rewarding
than pursuing an unwilling one.

He jammed the crowbar back into the mud-spat-
tered lilac and silver fender and gave it one more
good pry. "We'll have it good as new soon," he said
gruffly.

To give her credit, she was a far more complex
woman than he had thought. He didn't like complex, he reminded himself. Complex generally
meant emotional, and emotional generally led to
disaster. Keep personal life simple, academic life
complex.

He wondered if Will was feeling better.

"Good of you," Fuller said again. "Particularly
when you said you had a lecture to write for tomorrow."

"Blast the lecture," he grumbled. He couldn't
concentrate. After last week's debacle in the obser-

vatory, he'd been too annoyed to sleep and had spent the rest of the night working on his latest treatise. But even those efforts would likely need to be discarded. Disconnected, sentimental rubbish.

Today, again, he needed to get out of his chambers. Do something active. Get out into the air. His thoughts were too unfocused now to put them to paper.

He heard the crunch of steps on the gravel of the inn yard and felt the students draw themselves up to polite attention.

"Sir," he said, slightly surprised to see the thin, lantern-jawed form of the Master of Trinity College. Caldwell wiped off his hands before extending one for a handshake. "It's good to see you."

"I suppose this is the curricle that went into the hen coop?" The Master examined the equipage with distaste.

The boys nodded. Kittley had the temerity to grin.

Master Lord Berring ignored them, his narrow eyes pinned on John. "Perhaps, Caldwell, if you can tear yourself away, I might have a word with you."

Caldwell gave his clothes a cursory look to ensure he wasn't too disgraceful and followed the man out of the inn yard.

The Master cast a doubtful look at the inn itself and another at the stained wooden bench in front of it, and with a fastidious smoothing of the rich fabric of his scholar's gown, elected to stand.

"You're not wearing your robes, Professor," he said, picking off an invisible speck of lint.

"I'm sorry, sir. It's Saturday. I have no official duties, and I am not on university grounds." He said it respectfully, but the Master must have caught the impatient undertone. Caldwell saw his big jaw tighten.

"Your official duties do not cease on Friday, sir. You are always a representative of Trinity College. I am not impressed to find you fraternizing with the students, engaged in menial labor, and in general conducting yourself like a commoner rather than a gentleman of your standing."

"I'm sorry, sir," he said again, reminding himself that protest, just as in his school days, would cost him the adult equivalent of a box on the ears.

"Perhaps you don't appreciate the fact that your role here is rather tenuous. I took you on last year because of Hillyard's unexpected death, and because DeVaux recommended you. DeVaux comes from an exceedingly well-respected family. A real gentleman."

His significant nudge to the word *real* left Caldwell's ears ringing as though he had indeed received a blow.

"I believe, sir," he said instead, "that I was taken on by the college because of my academic credentials and not my bloodline."

The Master closed his eyes for a moment, then opened them again. "Indeed. Trinity is far more interested in your ability to educate our students than whether your father was nothing but a tuppence solicitor and your mother disowned for marrying him."

"I'm glad to hear it," he said dryly.

The great jaw thrust forward ominously. "However, we have often found that breeding and ability go hand in hand. And I must admit that it is your ability to educate that I am concerned about at present. Your tendency toward familiarity, your cavalier attitude—they have been noted and are not approved of."

Caldwell stood still, forcing his hands to remain still at his sides, his gaze impassive. No need to react, he reminded himself. Keep the personal life simple.

"Perhaps you have taken your lead from De-Vaux," the Master went on. "I am not pleased with him either, but his impeccable social standing makes him naturally hold himself more removed from the rabble." The man twitched his robes and observed with obvious satisfaction the way the glossy fabric fell back into place. "You, however, must constantly be vigilant. You must not seek to befriend the students. You should not take an interest in their lives outside of your lectures and your tutorial sessions. You certainly should not spend your Saturdays helping them repair their carriages."

The Master was warming to his topic, punctuating his oration with great swoops of his scholarly gown.

"No scandal must attach itself to your name," he went on. "You cannot afford it, I assure you. I should not like our patrons, the parents of our scholars, or even the fellows of other colleges to say that we engage anyone but the most upright, honorable, and high-minded men to act as fellows at Trinity College." The Master's fist prodded every attribute.

"I understand that, sir." There was nothing to be done at this point but let the lecture roll over him and wait for it to be done.

"Your youth is not in your favor," the Master continued. "Your background will be subjected to scrutiny. It is imperative that you keep your dis-

tance and keep your mind and heart on purely
scholarly pursuits."

"Except when it comes to securing large endowments for the college." He couldn't resist. He truly
couldn't.

"Your levity does you no credit," the jaw snapped.
"It is precisely what will be your undoing. I am giving you fair warning, Professor Caldwell."

Caldwell stood up straighter, determined not to
react. "I understand what you are saying, sir."

He felt the old urge to tell the pompous ass to go
to the devil. It wouldn't be the first time his breeding, his nature, and his dashed levity would cost
him his employment.

But this was different. This wasn't just a respectably dull clerk's position secured for him by
his family or some menial job taken on merely to
spite them. This was actually something he cared
about. Something, dash it all, that he was good at.

"Excellent," the Master said, apparently ap-
peased. "Perhaps spending less time with Professor
DeVaux would also be in order. I don't like my fellows to be dashing. I don't wish to hear of them
spoken of by giggling misses in the town. I hear
DeVaux's been getting love notes from the school-
girls at the seminary up the road. My fellows should
not wear London coats and boots rather than their
robes. Makes the college look like Bond Street
rather than a place of learning. Not that *your* coats
are made on Bond Street."

"I will wear the robes as you suggest, sir," Caldwell
ground out.

So Pratt could keep his mistress, Chesterfield his
beloved sherry, and Hart his predilection for gam-
bling. They had family names that overshadowed
even the most shocking of sins. Even DeVaux, blast

him, was above censure. While he himself had done nothing more than, well, than bring an unknown lady of mixed reputation to the observatory where he had attempted activities that perhaps would qualify as scandalous.

And truth to be told, if she had allowed it, he would have very much liked to have carried on with further pleasures that would have made the Master's lantern jaw drop.

The Master had continued to enumerate his various sins and was now winding to a close. He gave Caldwell a long, haughty stare to ensure that he understood. "I want solid, respectable men without a breath of scandal attached to their names. Men of repute. Do you understand me, Professor?"

It might as well have been his father talking. Respectable, always respectable. And, of course, respectably in one's place.

Caldwell twisted his face into a placating smile, disgusted that he was unable to respond. He mentally counted stars and reminded himself that the humiliation was worth it.

When at last the man sailed up the road, his black robes belled out like a funeral barge, Caldwell let his shoulders sink in a sigh of annoyance.

It was proving difficult to keep his personal life simple with the likes of the Master and Lady Whitcombe intruding. At least Lady Whitcombe's antipathy stemmed from his actions rather than his breeding. Dash it all, he couldn't really blame her. He'd shown up at her house and been abominably rude and nosy, then on their very next meeting attempted to seduce her.

He couldn't help but grin. Yes, she hated him, pure and simple. And one had to admire simplicity.

He reminded himself again that there were sev-

eral far more accommodating women than the fair
Lady Whitcombe. He also reminded himself that
he had a lecture to prepare. And that he should
go back to his rooms and don his dashed awkward
scholarly robes before the Master chucked him out.

His thoughts were cut short when a dashing lilac
and silver curricle came to a pawing, snorting stop
next to him.

"Ho!" shouted Boxty. "See, we have her on her
pins again." He struggled to control his spirited
pair as Kittley drew up with a great flourish in his
own smart carriage.

"Care to join us?" the young man asked. "Boxty
here has wagered a pony, poor fool, that his rattle-
trap affair, still covered in chicken feathers, can
beat my phaeton."

"Your cattle are touched in the wind," Caldwell
said mildly.

"They are not." Kittley looked wounded.

"Mad Jack paid a mountain of guineas for them,
but I told him at the time they were bellows to
mend," Boxty put in.

Caldwell gave the horses a critical once over.
"You'll do well enough if the race is short, but anything over two miles . . ."

"Nonsense. I'll beat Boxty over ten miles. I'll race
you to"—Kittley squinted at the signpost up the
road—"to Potton."

"You must come, Professor," Boxty urged. "How
else will we have someone to fairly call the race?"

If he valued his career, he would coolly tell the
boys to go about their games while he went back to
his lecture notes. And perhaps once he was done
with them, he would have time to work on his research. And then perhaps a glass of ale with pretty

Molly of the Three Tuns. This could be the perfect time to begin anew. Yes, a perfectly respectable plan.

In another moment, he had swung into Boxty's curricle. "As a matter of fact, I happened to be heading to Potton anyway."

Chapter Eight

"Mama," William said tentatively, his brown eyes barely appearing over the enormous pile of linen he was holding. "Why must we do spring cleaning now? It isn't really spring yet. You said so yourself when I went out without my coat yesterday."

Eleanor sat back from the linen closet and dropped her hands. Goodness but she'd been working in a fever. Little wonder William was looking at her as though she'd gone mad. "Well, it's very nearly spring," she said with a smile, "and we shall get it over with. Who wants to do spring cleaning when the weather is fine? We will feel so clever when everyone else is busy with spring cleaning, and we are already finished."

She held up the last of the sheets and inspected it for holes. Not the best quality, but it would have to do for another year.

"Everyone else has servants," William muttered.

Eleanor gave him a warning look. "Now put those in the pile for laundering and help me carry your bedroom rug outside."

He was right, though. There was no reason for this flurry of activity. She just needed to keep busy. It kept her from thinking too much. And after that night in the observatory, she'd had too much to think about.

William obediently helped her roll up the rug, and together they carried it out to where two others were strung on a line between two trees in the back garden.

"Now, your next job," she began, catching sight of his woeful expression, "is to go and amuse yourself however you like."

She laughed as he brightened immediately and raced off toward the brook, where he had been engaged yesterday in building a dam. She bit back the urge to call after him that he should be careful not to get his feet wet.

Instead, she picked up the rug beater from where she'd left it against a tree and went to work on the rug. It was enormously satisfying to see the great clouds of dust rise off of it with each thwack.

Clean. A new start. If she could not make her mind orderly, she could at least make her life so.

She found that her thoughts had been drawn back to the night in the observatory despite her efforts to avoid it. What had she been thinking, sobbing over Dr. Stalk's improper advances one moment, then throwing herself like a light skirt at Caldwell the next?

She'd wanted Caldwell to kiss her. Desperately. And worse was the fact that it was purely for the pleasure of it. She didn't even have the weak excuse that she thought herself in love with the man. Lord, worse, she actively disliked him. But even so, one moment alone with him, detested or not, and she was behaving as wantonly as in the days back in London.

She dealt the rug a violent blow. No, she wouldn't think about that.

She heard the faint sound of a door slam and looked up the hill to where the Castons' maid was dragging out a basket of laundry. Eleanor saw that the girl was looking at her so she waved, but the maid pretended not to see.

She turned back to the rug, determined not to feel wounded. The Caston family had always ignored her, and she had always appreciated it. After all, she'd moved to Potton to escape her past. She'd wanted the peace and anonymity of the countryside. She certainly hadn't been overly friendly with the neighbors. And while perhaps she hadn't been granted anonymity, she had peace.

She stepped back from the choking cloud of dust and drew a few deep breaths. Perhaps too much peace. She felt a bit, well, empty these days. And it had obviously affected her decision-making of late.

There was the sound of horses and the shouts of several men at the front of the cottage. What was Jordan doing here? He wasn't to visit until Thursday. And had he brought friends?

She looked down at her gray work gown covered with a serviceable linen smock. Perhaps it was only some travelers looking for directions. Jenny could deal with them.

But in another moment, Jenny appeared at the back door.

"Professor Caldwell, Lord Fuller, and Mr. Kittley to see you," she said, anxiously wrapping her hands in her apron. "Shall I tell him you aren't at home? You didn't give instructions as to what I should tell callers."

"We never have callers," Eleanor remarked. Oh, of all times to come visiting! Here she was, tip to toe in dust, with her hair hanging out of her cap. Fly away with the man, why now? And with friends? But if they'd come all the way from Cambridge, she couldn't very well tell them she wasn't at home to them.

But then again, to be presentable, she would have to have a full bath, and there was no time for that. Botheration.

As she stood there, uncharacteristically undecided, William came out of the house pulling Caldwell by the sleeve.

"Mama, I saw the carriages and went round to the front of the house. It's Professor Caldwell and some of the students from the university. You should see the carriages they arrived in. They're bang up to the mark. They had a race and Lord Fuller won. You should see his horses. I told them there was no need to sit in the drawing room as we never have callers, but that they should come straight out to us."

Will looked so pleased to be playing the host that she didn't have the heart to reprimand him. So there was nothing to be done but to shove the escaped hair back into the cap and make as dignified a curtsey as possible.

She raised her eyes to see that Caldwell, instead of wearing that impossible sardonic smile, looked slightly ruffled. "I'm sorry, madam," he stammered. "I can see that you're busy. We'll not interrupt you."

What, had he expected to find her reclining on a settee while servants fetched French novels and sweetmeats for her? She stood up straighter. Very well, let him see that she worked just as hard as any crofter, despite her grand title.

"Should we go?" the young man introduced as Lord Fuller asked. His lanky shoulders drooped in a boyish expression of contrition.

Eleanor dragged her gaze away from the rather

alarming combination of his bright blue coat and yellow trousers. Had he really worn a pink and orange striped waistcoat with them?

"Nonsense," she said with a smile. "Jenny will serve you tea. If you've come all the way from Cambridge you must be thirsty. Perhaps you would prefer a bit of Madeira? We will take our refreshment outside here in the garden, as the weather is rather fine. As you can see, I'm afraid my household cannot afford formality." Her guests likely had not expected to take tea in a vegetable garden, but it was much more pleasant than entertaining in the old-fashioned, overcrowded house.

The two students looked rather cheered at the mention of tea, but Caldwell bowed stiffly. "I would prefer there be no formality. But I do not wish to intrude where we are not welcome."

He really was shockingly handsome. Perhaps she deserved a bit of credit for resisting him in the observatory after all. DeVaux was perhaps better looking, with his broad shoulders and his serious, brooding looks. Caldwell, however, with his over-long hair, his decided chin, and his oddly changeable hazel eyes had a far more potent appeal.

She realized with a start that she had been staring and had not responded. She was launching into a stupid response as to how welcome they were when Will saved her.

"I have been building a dam in the brook. Will you come and see it?" he asked, the perfect country squire. "Afterward we might have a bit of cake, couldn't we, Mama? Jenny makes a very good iced cake. I'm not often allowed to have any, unless we have visitors. I hope you will come again quite often."

The two gentlemen appeared far more interested in the dam than in cake, and accepted his invitation to see his newest feat of engineering. Will led them away with grave ceremony, but Caldwell hung back with a limping excuse of helping Jenny with the tea things.

"You'd do better to go see William's dam," Eleanor said sharply, picking up the rattan beater again. "Jenny needs no help, and I must finish these rugs." She was still rather unreasonably cross with him for daring to appear when she looked such a fright.

In her fantasies—for now she could admit that she had had them—the next time she had seen him after the scene in the observatory, she had been regal, composed, distant. Certainly not head to toe in dirt.

"I will help you," he said, coming toward her.

"No." She put the rug beater behind her back, irrationally convinced he meant to snatch it from her. "You'll spoil your fine coat." She went around to the other side of the rug and began beating it enthusiastically, hoping to convince him of how very busy she was.

He gave a little cough, whether from the dust or from nervousness she could not tell. "Lady Whitcombe," he said from his side of the rug at last, "there is something I would like to discuss."

Lady Whitcombe. She hated the way he said it, drawing out the words, making them sound like some false, pompous affectation. And of course he knew very well by now that, title or not, she was anything but ladylike.

"I don't believe there is anything we need to discuss," she said firmly. "Have things been going well at the university?"

There was silence from the other side of the rug for a moment.

"I have been thinking of you a great deal."

Oh dear. He sounded like a man who was about to confess something. Was he so sentimental that after that odd moment of weakness in the observatory he thought himself in love with her? Impossible. He was a man of sense. Still, perhaps he wasn't made of wood after all. Perhaps he did feel the same attraction for her that she felt for him. Perhaps he was as confused as she was about what had passed between them.

"I am appalled and ashamed of my behavior last week. I took advantage of you in a moment of distress. I must apologize."

She dragged her runaway mind to an abrupt halt. That hardly sounded like the confession of a man burning with passion.

It didn't matter. There was only one rational answer. "I'm certain we can forget what happened. It was late. We were both quite tired." She began thwacking away at the rug again. There. The conversation was closed.

Again, a short silence. She resisted the urge to peep around the rug to make certain he was still there.

"I am not a man of pretty words," he said very quietly at last. "And I am not a man with a passionate nature. I don't know what came over me to act so out of character."

Her arm stilled in mid strike. Clearly not her charms. It was a bit ungentlemanly to let her know he regretted it quite so much. She'd lain awake half the night wishing she'd let him kiss her. Now, she was wholeheartedly glad she had not. "The matter is forgotten," she said firmly.

"Excellent," he said, suddenly cheerful. As though that really was all it took to forget the matter entirely. "Let's take a turn in the garden."

She put down the beater and came around the rug. The horrid man wore his twisted smile again, mocking her, or perhaps them both.

Lord, but he was difficult to read! It was as though he knew very well that it was impossible for her to break her years of ladylike training and tell him to go to the devil. She took his arm just as he must have known she would, and they walked the perimeter of the garden.

They must have looked a pretty picture. A ridiculous promenade with her in her work clothes, her hair untidy and her smock streaked with dirt. And there he was, brushed and clean and handsome as no man had a right to be in his splendid blue superfine coat and brown and gold waistcoat.

They walked for a few moments in silence. Heavens, but this was as bad as the sarcasm.

"Do you ever leave this house, Lady Whitcombe?"

She turned to look at him, not wholly convinced he was not making fun of her. She gave him what she hoped was a cool, dignified smile. "Of course I do. You've seen me in Cambridge twice."

"I mean, do you ever leave for pleasure?"

She noted that there were a few last turnips forgotten under the straw bedding covering the ground. She must remember to dig them up later. "We enjoyed the sledding."

"Do you ever go out socially for your own enjoyment?"

She looked at him in some confusion. "I'm not sure what you mean. If you are asking whether I ever go to assemblies or to salons or things like that, no, I'm afraid I don't."

"Why not?" He looked genuinely surprised.

"Why not?" she echoed. Did the man grasp nothing of her social position? "There is no need to play ignorant, Professor Caldwell. You know very well why I do not go about in public."

He had the bad grace to laugh at her. "No, no, anything but the freezing glance. I cannot bear that. You must remember that my heart is not as strong as a member's of the *beau monde*."

"Impossible man." She could not help but laugh as well. "If you put on the East London accent I shall be forced to have Jenny eject you from the house as so much rabble."

Trust Caldwell to view her past as though it were merely . . . well, the past. "Perhaps I have not gone out in public because there is nothing offered in the sleepy hamlet of Potton that is tempting to a viscountess like myself."

He moaned and pretended to stagger. His dramatics brought his broad shoulder in contact with her own, but she didn't really mind. Actually, it was rather lovely to take a turn in the garden with a gentleman escort. Even if the garden was only a vegetable patch and the gentleman was only Professor Caldwell.

"Yes, I can see that," he said. "Better to rot here like your turnips than be known to be a member of an inferior Ladies' Literary Society."

"Oh, absolutely," she said. He was still horrid, of course, and his sarcasm was abominable, but she had to give him credit for mocking everyone, even himself, with equal vigor. "Is there a Ladies' Literary Society?" she asked rather shyly at last.

"Why yes," he said. "Lady Reed has presided over one for years now. It's considered rather good, I believe. Though quite radical in its notions on feminine education, divorce, and voting. Lady Reed is a bit of a dissenter at heart."

Lady Reed. She repeated the name in her head with the same emphasis on *Lady* that Caldwell himself was wont to use. Not a circle that would welcome her, radical ideas or not. She felt suddenly rather annoyed with Caldwell. His feelings of social inferiority were all in his head. Hers were quite real.

"Perhaps not quite my style," she said with exaggerated loftiness.

"Then what is? What would tempt you from your cloister here?"

"Oh well, nothing too intellectual of course," she continued with a flippant wave of her hand. "I'm quite a frivolous character, you know. So anything at Cambridge is out of the question. Lecture series and such would make me break out in hives. And I couldn't be thought a bluestocking, of course." She made a courtly gesture with the narrow skirts of her work gown. "Perhaps something that involved wasting a great deal of money."

"Or perhaps a ball?" His eyes were full of laughter.

"Yes indeed, a ball would do it. But only the grandest kind. None of your subscription affairs with warm lemonade and nabobs' daughters."

"Oh, certainly, nothing like that," he agreed. He really did look mischievous when he grinned. "A pompous kind of ball. With knee breeches required. And of course, at least three waltzes, lobster patties, Champagne, and a hostess who looks down her nose every bit as well as you do."

She could not help laughing with him. "Yes, something like that would do very well indeed. Assuming of course that there was a card room with very high stakes. And an enormous number of silly young men who would pay me extravagant compliments."

"Excellent," he said. "Then you will come with me to the Trinity Easter Term Ball."

"What?" She half thought he was joking, but he seemed, for once, quite complacent.

"Come to the ball," he said again.

"I was merely jesting, Professor Caldwell," she said, suddenly feeling a little self-conscious. "I wouldn't be able to go to a ball. Of any sort." She was rather ashamed to find herself surprised and even rather pleased that he'd invited her. He wished for her company after all then.

"Nonsense," he said. "It will do you good. Mind you, I've misled you a bit, as it truly will be a deadly dull affair. I've been told that every year is the same as the last, right down to the tunes the orchestra plays. They say the Master's wife has been wearing the same pink turban for four years running." There was a curve to his mouth that reminded her of Will when he was about to start trying to convince her of something. "It is guaranteed to be an ordeal of the first water. But you really must go."

A ball. When was the last time she had been to a ball? Or any social outing? At least nine years. She realized that instead of carefully formulating her reasons why she could not possibly go, her selfish mind had raced on to ransack her wardrobe for the occasion. Fortunately, this had the same dampening effect.

"Indeed, I must not go. I am not respectable," she said firmly. "And you know it very well. I could not go to formal functions like your ball, even if I wanted to."

He pretended to think for a moment, but she

could see his eyes glittering under the half-closed lids. "Mayhaps I don't understand the ways of the gentry like," he said at last, in the strongest of East London accents. "But I cannot see that 'ere in Cambridge, an incident wot 'appened nine years ago would matter overmuch. Ye'ud 'ave to think fair 'igh of yerself to think everyone's eyes and minds are turned to you all of a time."

"Lud, anything but the accent!" she exclaimed. Then, when his eyes remained seriously upon her, she dropped her gaze to his shining Hessians. Her own half boots looked very sadly scuffed in comparison. "Perhaps I *am* vain. Perhaps you're right, and it is self-absorption that keeps me so reclusive. But," she looked up at him, "truly I cannot. Literary societies are one thing, but a ball? I would not be comfortable. I live a very retired life now."

"It's because you're still angry with me," he said, looking quite genuinely disappointed.

"Nonsense. It—"

"It's because you are ashamed to be seen at a ball with a man of such grotesque origins as myself." He pulled a mournful face.

"Oh, do stop being ridiculous."

"It's because you are afraid."

"Oh, really . . ." She rolled her eyes scornfully.

She could see Will and the two university students coming back from the stream. Lord Fuller had one very wet trouser leg.

"Then say you will go," Caldwell said with a shrug. "It serves a great many purposes. I will believe you have forgiven me for the debacle of last week, and you will prove that you bear no ill will toward me despite the fact that I've tortured you with my accent. You will show the world that you are not afraid to go out in public and confirm in your own mind that no one gives a hang about some old London rumors. And," he finished triumphantly, "you can give me a really stinging set-down in public should I acquire any notion that we are anything beyond the coolest of acquaintances."

He gave her a wheedling smile, much more boyish and open than the sarcastic one. "Just think how efficient."

"Tempting," she said with her best look of highbred scorn. Then she gave a regretful laugh. "But I cannot. Truly. Thank you very much for your offer, but I assure you it is not a possibility."

"So you'll consider it," he nodded. He turned to take the tea tray from Jenny as the girl, rather flushed and frazzled looking at the appearance of so much company, struggled to move an enormous amount of food out onto the lawn. "Goodness, I must congratulate you. You have provided enough food even for these young gentlemen. You will have won their hearts and affection forever." He greeted Will and the young men and watched with evident pride as they sat ravenously down to the dishes Jenny had provided.

Eleanor continued to bounce feeble protests off his back until at last he looked over his shoulder. "Excellent. It is decided then. I shall send a carriage for you next Saturday evening at eight."

Chapter Nine

When the carriage drew up in front of the little cottage the night of the ball, John was still not entirely certain that Eleanor would attend. After his high-handed assumption that she would accept, he deserved it if she'd decided to go out for the evening and leave him high and dry.

And, if truth be told, he was not entirely certain why he'd asked her. It had been an impulsive thing to do, and he was not, in general, an impulsive man. Irresponsible, perhaps. Irreverent, most assuredly. But not impulsive.

It would have been much simpler, after all, to allow Lady Whitcombe to continue living her retired life, and to continue on with his own academic pursuits. That route would have pleased the Master, pleased Lady Whitcombe, and pleased himself.

But no, some mad notion had made him ask Lady Whitcombe, and after all his ridiculous teasing her to come, he couldn't very well cry off.

The woman who answered the door was not the Eleanor Whitcombe he knew. It was a luminous, alarmingly beautiful stranger, unrecognizable except for the familiar expression of cool reserve.

He'd never seen Eleanor wear anything other

than black or gray. Work clothes, morning gowns, carriage dresses—they were all dark and puritanically severe. Now she stood in the doorway, her moon-pale ball gown illuminating the small, dark entryway of the cottage.

"You look lovely," he said, trying to match her unconcern. He pretended to adjust his jacket and not ogle her. After all, he was an educated, rational adult. "Really. Very pretty." No, no. He sounded like some adolescent moonling who'd never seen an attractive woman before. He tried desperately to think of something urbane, light. Flattering, but not lascivious.

He'd never seen such white skin. Her neck, shoulders, and arms were pale and smooth as chalk. He'd seen ladies in much more revealing ball gowns, of course. But such a modest expanse of naked skin looked quite remarkable after she'd kept it hidden for so long.

He stared as she took up her cloak and reticule and pulled the door closed behind her. When she took his arm, he was tempted to check to see if she left a pale sparkling powder of her essence behind on his sleeve.

Lord, little wonder she'd been pursued in London. The sensuality of her beauty, its almost wanton voluptuousness, paired with her still, cool reserve was enough to drive a man mad.

"Excellent," he said gruffly. "Shall we go then? Because we are rather late. Not that it is necessary to rush, of course." Devil fly away with it, he was hardly intelligible, never mind urbane.

He rather wished her back into her black casing so they could be comfortable again. But now she really did look like the grand London lady. And he felt, more than ever, the bourgeois Cheapsider.

"Do they know I'm coming?" she asked, breaking the silence in the carriage at last.

"They?" he echoed stupidly.

"The heads of Trinity. Did you tell them it was me you intended to invite?"

They, the heads of the college, did not know. It wasn't the sort of thing that came up in conversation. He hadn't considered asking their permission on something so ridiculous. This was a political event at heart, and whom one escorted was of little import. Besides, this was Cambridge. Eleanor's little scandal had doubtless been forgotten years ago in London. Intellectual, unfashionable Cambridge had most certainly never heard of her at all.

"Lady Whitcombe," he said sternly, "people will begin to think you are self-absorbed if you are always convinced that the world is talking about you. Did you expect a welcoming committee outside of the gates?"

To his surprise, rather than laugh at him or give him the stinging set-down he'd intended to provoke, she looked slightly chastened.

"Of course not," she said. "It's just—it's just that it has been a rather long time since I've been out in society. You're right. It is vain of me to think I will cause any stir in the least. I'm no one now."

Oddly, this seemed to cheer her a bit.

There had always been an air of raw sensuality about her. But tonight he realized that she was actually a genuinely beautiful woman. Of course he'd found her intriguing, attractive, striking. But now? Her rich chestnut hair, usually pulled severely back and hidden under a cap, was bare and swept up to a crown of curls. She was rather younger than he'd thought, he realized in some surprise. Perhaps only six and twenty. And in her simple, pale gown she looked so very innocent. And so maddeningly tempting.

He suddenly felt rather itchy in his starched evening clothes. It would have been so much more comfortable to merely sit at home tonight and work on his treatise. Perhaps play a tune on the violin, if things became too unbearable. This, however, was more than he had bargained for.

He tamped down the discomforting notion that his father might dislodge himself from behind the carriage seat and lean over to whisper in his ear that he had no business courting his betters and that he would get along a sight more comfortably if everyone just remembered his duty and his place.

Not that he was courting the lady, of course.

He fervently wished Lady Whitcombe had decided to wear her usual dowdy cap over those burnished curls.

But the carriage had drawn up to the grand hall, and he had little choice but to take the transformed woman by the hand, help her from the coach, and lead her into the ballroom.

She drew a bit closer to him, and he could feel the hand on his arm tremble a little. Good, it distracted him from the satyr of lust that had suddenly possessed him. Bad, her closeness brought an intoxicating scent of jasmine.

"Will Jordan be here?" she asked.

He realized with a start of embarrassment that he'd nearly forgotten she even knew DeVaux. He recalled his friend's warning about courting her. Not that he was courting her.

"He does not generally attend these things," Caldwell said with a shrug. "Loaned us his carriage, though." He didn't mention that DeVaux had loaned him his coat as well. When had he ever dreamed he would have need of a formal evening jacket? Not his line at all. "I'm afraid you'll just have to survive the evening without him." He watched her expression carefully, but she did not react.

He helped her out of her cloak, clumsily careful not to touch her skin, and then escorted her to the line of dons and their wives who were receiving. She might be nervous, but she was in her element far more than he. She must have gone to hundreds of balls in London. Little wonder she projected an air of serene elegance.

The nape of her neck looked so vulnerable with her hair swept up. He could see where the smooth column of her neck curved to meet the line of vertebrae in her back before disappearing coyly into the pale silk of her gown. Like a curious child, he wanted to touch them.

"Caldwell," the Master said, looking his coat over with an expression of grudging approval. "Glad you've finally decided to start participating in the genteel aspects of university life." His smile cut a slice from his narrow face. "And you have brought such an elegant guest."

"Lord Berring," he said with a pardonable surge of self-satisfaction, "may I introduce you to Lady Whitcombe?"

The Master took her hand, his eyes narrowed as he tried to recollect something. But it was his wife's pink-turbaned head that snapped toward them immediately.

"Whitcombe?" she repeated. "Eleanor Whitcombe?" John thought for a moment that he was about to witness the reunion of long-lost school friends or some such thing, but instead there was silence.

"Yes," said Eleanor at last. "I am Eleanor Whit-combe."

"Indeed." The woman raised her lorgnette and examined Eleanor from head to toe. "Indeed," she said again. "How singular."

Eleanor bowed to her, but the Master's wife did not offer her hand but instead drew back with an expression of distaste.

Beside him, he could feel Eleanor stiffen, but this was not the time to talk. He ignored Lady Berring's rudeness and nudged Eleanor forward through the line. Whatever had just happened must be glossed over. Fortunately, there were plenty of other ladies here who would not have such a memory for gossip.

Some of the dons were obviously ignorant as to her identity and some looked at her in surprise, but there was no doubt from the increase in murmurs behind them that everyone in their wake now knew her entire scandalous past. This was not how things were supposed to go.

"Ah," he said with forced joviality. "There is Reed. He teaches classics. His wife is quite the bluestocking. The Ladies' Literary Society, as you recall. I do hope we have the chance to speak with them."

She said nothing, her chin high and her eyes fixed.

"And there is Jack Kittley," he went on, trying to distract her. "I see he's brought his sister. Very high-spirited girl. Always throwing herself at poor Boxty Fuller. Ah yes, there is Boxty, in the striped waistcoat. Lord, it's awful. I told you they would all be here. No one misses it.

"Toby Eckles there assists me with my research. Bright student. Too bad about his taste in coats. Can I get you some orgeat?" He was nattering, he knew it. But what else was to be done when the wave of gossip was washing inexorably down the length of the room and everyone behind it had turned to stare?

"I hear the orgeat is notoriously weak and warm," he continued, "but I'm not certain what else is on offer."

"Orgeat would be fine," she said. She had gotten rather red in two spots on her cheeks, but she was quite calm. Her arrogant look was standing her in good stead tonight. She looked utterly unapproachable.

Boxty and Jack, bless them, were immune to both the rising murmurs in the room and Eleanor's chilly expression of disdain. With a look of delight they bounced over to the punch table.

"I say, Lady Whitcombe. Didn't recognize you," Kittley began. "Didn't realize you were so dashed pretty. Those black clothes you always wear quite disguise it."

"You look like"—Boxty groped for a moment—"a star. Yes, that's it. A star. All silvery. Wouldn't you say that, Professor Caldwell? Appropriate, eh?"

Caldwell scowled and drew Eleanor's arm through his. The insolent puppies were coming on a bit strong.

"You will dance with me?" Jack asked, all eagerness. "They are about to start. I promised my sister that I would dance with her if no one else would, but she's asked Boxty, so it's all right."

"You'll dance with me after that?" Boxty interrupted. "I'll make them play a waltz."

As much as Caldwell approved of their enthusiasm to make her feel welcome, it apparently hadn't occurred to the students that he himself might wish to dance with the woman he'd escorted. Though perhaps the delay would give him a chance to recall the steps he'd so laboriously learned last night. He found himself unexpectedly cross that *Mrs. Garfield's Elementary Introduction to the Country Dances* quite frowned on the waltz.

The room was now shining with lorgnettes and quizzing glasses, all trained on Eleanor. Caldwell saw her throat move as she swallowed; then she nodded and allowed Kittley to drag her into the set that was forming.

"Didn't recognize her," Boxty said, echoing his friend. "Heard Lady Berring say you'd brought a fancy woman," he went on thoughtfully. "Perhaps she didn't recognize Lady Whitcombe either."

The Master's wife recognized her all right. That was the problem. And now he'd exposed Eleanor to the very censorship and scorn she dreaded. Every guest at the ball was watching her dance with Kittley, whispering behind their fans and giving smirking glances.

"Lady Whitcombe's past is none of our business," he said coldly.

He'd make it up to her. Devil take it, she was a lady. More than anyone else in the room, she was a lady. And he'd flog anyone who said differently.

"Oh, I know." Boxty shrugged. "Don't know why there's such a fuss. After all, she's good fun. Much more fun than most of the ladies here. And there's hardly a one without some kick in her gallop. When it comes to their past, I mean." The boy gave Caldwell an unexpectedly knowing look. "Won't say more, but I could name ten ladies here who aren't strictly obeying the commandments. Pots calling the kettle black." He frowned at a woman with suspiciously brassy blond hair and took another swig of punch. "Odd that DeVaux isn't here."

"DeVaux?"

Boxty drew up his shoulders in his characteristic shrug. "Well, you'd think he would be here to quiet things down. The gossip, I mean. After all, he's the father."

The boy's nonsensical chatter was beginning to grate on Caldwell's nerves. "What are you going on about?" he demanded.

"William. Isn't that what all this fuss is about? The fact that DeVaux, and not Lord Whitcombe, is William's father?"

Caldwell's breath lodged awkwardly in his throat. There was a roar in his ears that made the musicians sound far away and tinny.

"DeVaux?" he said again. His voice sounded as strange as the music.

Clarity doused him with a cold shock. How stupid he'd been. He knew of course that Eleanor and De-Vaux knew each other from years back, but—. Of course. And Eleanor had not said a word.

Fuller edged behind a pillar, casting nervous glances toward where Jack Kittley's sister was searching the room for him.

"I thought you knew," Boxty said. "I thought everyone knew. It isn't as though DeVaux hid it. Dash it all, she's seen me. Now I'm done for."

Caldwell recalled the many visits, the kind attention, DeVaux's solicitous care of William. He'd been so blind not to see it. He felt a bit as though he would be ill. A bit as though he were going to go mad.

He realized now that he had been deceiving himself. For all his protestations of keeping his life simple, he'd developed a bit of a *tendre* for Eleanor. He'd entertained notions of—good Lord—perhaps even seriously paying court to the woman.

But she was DeVaux's woman.

He drained a glass of the vile orgeat, trying to order his racing thoughts. But, if Eleanor was De-Vaux's mistress, what the hell was she doing with him tonight?

Jack Kittley's sister belatedly claimed Fuller, and the young man allowed himself to be dragged onto the floor. It was already growing unbearably hot; the small room was pulsating with fluttering fans. His shirt points wilting in the heat, Caldwell remained woodenly at the punch table.

He looked around. The hall was decked out in silk flowers, the same ones as last year, most likely. And it was the same faces, the same couples parading themselves as though this really were some fine event. He'd put in an appearance last year, just to have his coat criticized and his presence snubbed. This year, of course, was different. Ah yes, he was the center of attention. The man who had come to the ball escorting Jordan DeVaux's mistress.

I thought you knew. I thought everyone knew. It isn't as though DeVaux hid it. He was such a fool.

The country dance wound to a close at last, and Kittley obediently escorted Eleanor back to the punch table where Caldwell still stood, her watery glass of orgeat still in his hand. As she approached, several couples moved away, tittering.

She was slightly flushed from the exercise but resolutely maintained her cool demeanor in the face of the curious murmurs.

"My turn," said Boxty, unceremoniously handing Miss Kittley back to her brother. "Lady Whitcombe, Mad Jack and I have loads of friends who would be glad to dance with you. You will not lack for partners, I assure you."

Eleanor gave Boxty the only genuine smile of the

evening. "You are good, Lord Fuller," she said warmly. "That would indeed make this ordeal easier to bear."

Caldwell couldn't stand this anymore. He took her arm. It was marble cold above her long white glove. "I must speak with you," he said.

Her brows arched higher in an expression of unmistakable scorn. "Sir, there can be no reason to talk. You knew what would happen when you brought me here. I presume this is meant as a great joke to put me in my place."

"What the—no!" He pulled her out into the cool night air of the courtyard. It was reviving after the closeness of the ballroom. Above them, the stars were spectacular, even the faintest clear and visible. He wanted to look up at them, assess them, use them as his touchstone to make himself calm, rational again. But now was not the time.

"Is DeVaux your lover?" he blurted.

She looked taken aback, then quickly retreated behind her emotionless mask. "I presume you mean Jordan? No."

He was spinning out of control. This evening, his whole acquaintance with Lady Whitcombe should have been only a mild amusement. Just something for him to do, and a little encouragement for the sad-eyed widow to get out more. Why should he give a hang about her romantic affairs?

"No?" he echoed breathlessly. "Then why—then who is William's—"

"I choose not to discuss these things with strangers," she said in a brittle voice.

"Strangers?" For some reason this wounded him more than anything that had come before. "Eleanor, I thought—well, I thought we were friends."

The night breeze caught the diaphanous layers of her gown and lifted them, teased them apart into filmy wings. Their fluttering was in odd contrast to her body's utter stillness. "Was bringing me here one of your jokes? Another way to show me how proud I am?"

"No," he said urgently. "I didn't realize people would remember your past. I had no idea people would be so cruel and hypocritical as to judge you for it after all this time." He took her by the shoulders and looked anxiously into her face to see if she believed him. If nothing else, that much was important.

She lifted her chin, her expression unreadable. "Then I'm sorry my presence was an embarrassment to you. I should have known how it would be. It was silly to have hoped otherwise. And I genuinely regret it if my accepting your invitation has damaged your reputation in any way."

He was about to reply that this was a ridiculous notion, when he was interrupted by the silent appearance of the Master, the man's expression of displeasure so severe that he could have cut stone with his sharp cheekbones.

"Professor Caldwell," he said, crossing his arms over his chest, "I am sorry you did not let us know whom you intended to invite to our ball. We certainly assumed that you knew what was appropriate. I'm afraid your choice of companion has greatly offended many of the ladies present. Not the least of whom is the hostess, my wife. I am certain you will understand if I request that you remove this person from the premises."

Caldwell opened his mouth, then closed it again, trying to keep his temper in check. Telling this pompous windbag just what he thought of him would not help Eleanor. Nor his own future at Trinity.

"You may speak to me if you are going to speak of me," Eleanor said unexpectedly. She looked down her nose at Berring, every inch a viscountess. "And I shall take my leave when I choose. I have as much right to civil treatment here as anyone."

"Get her out of here," the Master commanded, still not looking at her.

John knew he should be heroic. He should smash the Master's beak of a nose and call him out for insulting Lady Whitcombe. But a voice in his head reminded him that she was DeVaux's woman. She was under Jordan's protection, not his. And the lady wanted nothing to do with his attempted heroics at all.

"To cast stones at a woman like myself, who has no family and no husband to shield her, that must make you feel very important, Lord Berring." Eleanor's voice was low and calm.

The Master's lips had disappeared under the pressure of his jaw, and there was a thick bifurcated vein pulsing in his wide forehead. He looked like a steam engine about to explode.

"Mmm." Eleanor closed her eyes and tilted her head. "A minuet. You will dance with me, Caldwell?"

He stared at her for a moment, then recovered himself enough to offer his arm and move toward the dance floor. He looked over his shoulder to see the Master standing with his arms dangling helplessly, sputtering.

"You were brilliant," he said warmly. "Absolutely brilliant. Said exactly what I wished I'd—"

"One dance and then I'd like to go home." Eleanor's voice was sharp. "I must make my point, but I don't fancy being on show for the rest of the evening."

He continued to try to praise her, but her expression was set, pleasant but unhearing.

"Eleanor, don't lump me in with all these petty, shallow people. Blame it on my ignorance of high society. Blame it on my ignorance, full stop. I had no idea people would recall some stupid rumors after so long." DeVaux's woman or not, it suddenly seemed vitally important that she not think badly of him.

He knew he'd disappointed her. A man like De-Vaux would have defended her, damn the consequences. He would have done more than shuffle awkwardly through the movements of the minuet. DeVaux would have run them all through or challenged them all to duels or some such dramatic, gentlemanly act of the Mayfair set.

But he, selfishly thinking of his own skin, had done nothing. "Don't think I did this knowingly," he said. "Don't think—"

She looked at him, but despite her smile, her eyes were emotionless. "It really doesn't matter what I think," she said.

Chapter Ten

"But Mrs. Agby," Lady Reed put her teacup back into the saucer with a dramatic rattle, "I'm certain you don't mean that Miss Wollstonecraft's principle itself is wrong."

The other ladies of the literary salon gave small murmurs of disapproval.

"Not in the least." Mrs. Agby gasped and pressed a hand to her bosom. "I merely meant that I regret that the moral decisions she made in her personal life have in some ways undermined her cause by making her an easy target for wholesale dismissal."

The late March rain hissed down the chimney and made the fire in Eleanor's little sitting room belch faint black clouds of ash. Well versed in the necessary procedure after several weeks of meetings, Mrs. Gregory waved Eleanor back into her seat and went to open the window and jiggle the chimney damper.

Lady Reed sighed. "Indeed. An interesting point, and one I know we've all given much thought to. I myself have wished on occasion that Wollstonecraft's pursuit of equal education for women had not been paired with her tenet that marriage is not a sacred state. After all, there is no reason that women cannot be educated like men but still be their equal partners in marriage. Her own illegitimate child by Imlay and her vigorous pursuit of him after the relationship had ended only holds her up to ridicule. Indeed, her personal life is used by some to emphasize the frailty of women and their utter lack of judgment and responsibility despite any education." She looked at the notes she had made in a bound morocco leather book and shook her head.

"Lady Whitcombe," she went on, "you are an educated gentlewoman as well as one who followed the Wollstonecraft tenet that love is more important than a traditional marriage arrangement. Do you have any words of defense for Wollstonecraft?"

Eleanor smiled and poured out a bit more tea to those who required it in the small group of women assembled in her sitting room. How strange, and how refreshing that her past, which of course everyone knew, could be approached without euphemisms and sidewinding.

"Indeed I don't," she said. "While I do feel strongly that Wollstonecraft is correct in her assessment of feminine intelligence and capability, I do not think that marriage should be dispensed with, nor do I think that impermanent liaisons made merely for pleasure are often truly equal. There is almost always one who is left wounded when it is dissolved."

Miss Jennings, a clever, well-read girl despite her young years, looked up in surprise. "But Lady Whitcombe," she protested, "surely you believe that love transcends marriage. You, of all people."

Eleanor looked around the group of women, who had, in the last month, become more loyal and steadfast friends than she had ever known. "You all know my past," she said frankly. "And it is similar to

Wollstonecraft's in some ways, in that I bore a child by a man not my husband. But she made her choices as a single, unmarried woman. I, as you know, was not. My marriage to Whitcombe was arranged and entirely loveless, it is true. But because I was self-indulgent, because I gave free rein to my emotions, my selfish whims, I shamed my family and myself and ultimately put myself in a position of far more misery than that of a loveless marriage."

Miss Jennings looked almost betrayed in her disappointment. "But you were in love," she protested. "And even though perhaps you now look on your decision with bitterness because it did not end well, surely at the time you felt—"

Eleanor smiled. "It sounds like sour grapes, does it not?" She smoothed her gray wool gown over her knees and tried to collect her thoughts. "I don't believe now that I loved the man who contributed to my downfall. How can you ever tell? Because you *think* you're in love, does that mean that you genuinely are? Because the feeling goes away, does that mean that it wasn't real in the first place?"

Miss Jennings bit her lip and looked down into her tea. "I have never fallen in love. So I don't know."

Eleanor looked out the window to where she could see William building tomato frames for his garden. "I don't believe I have either," she said at last. "At least, not the romantic love you speak of. I believe what I felt was merely rebellion and a self-indulgence of emotion. I did not wish to be married to Whitcombe. I wished to make my own choice. So I did. Unfortunately, that alliance was no better a match than my marriage."

She lifted her shoulders. "So my disagreement

with Mary Wollstonecraft is not that marriage is an outdated institution or that love is unimportant. I merely believe that duty and honor should come before personal indulgence. Passion is a selfish emotion."

Miss Jennings looked somewhat deflated, but Eleanor reached out and pressed her hand. "I think one can have it all," she said. "I just do not believe that passion should be the first consideration." She looked around at the slightly surprised faces in the drawing room and realized that it was the first time she had ever spoken so much to the group.

How different she must seem from the timid shadow of a woman who had so gingerly approached Lady Reed to ask if she might join the Ladies' Literary Society.

She watched as Mrs. Agby and Lady Reed took up opposite ends of the debate and tugged it back and forth between them.

Caldwell had been right. In this one thing at least. It had been time to forgive herself, and to move back into some sort of society. And while there were those in the community who would never accept her, there were others who paid no heed to old scandal.

Caldwell. At least she had not let passion get the better of her there. Which was certainly for the best. After that wretched ordeal of the Easter Term Ball, he had not come calling again.

She did not feel as satisfied as she wished.

Outside the window she saw William look up and grin, then race off toward the gravel drive. She was ashamed to find her heart beating faster. Perhaps he had come calling at last after all.

Passion is self-indulgence, she repeated to herself. And really, once it was excised, one truly hardly missed it.

She sat up straighter, pretending unconcern when Jenny came in to announce the visitor. The woman bent over and murmured a name in her ear. "DeVaux?" she repeated, then realized she sounded disappointed.

"Professor DeVaux," Lady Reed exclaimed, far more delighted. "Excellent. Do let him in." She nodded approvingly to the other ladies. "You have a good friend there, Eleanor. A real gentleman. He'll make someone who *isn't* opposed to marriage"—she gave Mrs. Agby a meaningful look—"an excellent husband someday."

Eleanor opened her mouth to protest, but De-Vaux entered the room and the ladies turned at once to greet him.

"Lady Whitcombe," he said, once he had exchanged pleasantries with the other ladies and accepted a piece of cake and a cup of tea. "You have become a very busy woman. I called on Monday, but you were at a musical lecture, and on Thursday, but you were at a meeting of the circulating library committee."

"I'm sorry not to have been at home."

"Nonsense. I'm delighted to find you're doing more. You know how long I've been badgering you to make more friends, go out more, and stop living as if this is a cloister."

She laughed. "Well, I finally began to agree with you."

"Excellent. That fits in perfectly with my plan. Lady Reed is hosting a star-watching evening." He bowed his head to that woman. "I am to lecture. We'd both hoped that you and William would go."

"Oh," she said. This would be her first encounter

with people at the university since the disaster of the Easter Term Ball. "I'm not certain I would be welcome."

He knew of course what had happened at that august gathering. Everyone knew.

He shrugged and made a dismissive gesture. "The kind of people who would not welcome you are not the kind of people who are invited," he said. "You know most of them anyway. People from the historical lecture series and the Classics Society. It was Lady Reed who suggested we host an evening explaining the classical roots of the constellations."

It did indeed sound tempting. Though she wondered if perhaps she was becoming rather too much the social butterfly. There was rarely an afternoon when she did not attend some function, generally with Will. Perhaps it was too much. But it had been so freeing, finally, after nine years to begin to loosen the constraints she'd put on her life.

For all her mixed emotions regarding Caldwell, he had been right about that. Rather embarrassingly, she had to admit that he was part of the reason she hesitated now.

She walked to the window, putting some distance between herself and the group of women. "Are you the only one lecturing?" she asked. "None of the other professors?" She pretended great interest in the progress of the tomato frames.

DeVaux sensed her desire for privacy and followed her to the window. "Yes, we didn't want it to go all night. It will start quite late as it is."

She relaxed a little. "Very well. I would love to attend. I have never seen you lecture. Are you certain though that people will not talk?" She lowered her voice. "It is one thing for you to occasionally be seen here. But to be seen with Will and me in public? You know people— Well, it seems a bit too cavalier about public opinion."

DeVaux lifted his shoulders in his usual inscrutable fashion. "Just biddies talking too much," he said scornfully. "And better for people to know you're under my protection than alone in the world."

They both fell silent for a moment. "Speaking of women reluctant to accept my protection," Jordan went on with a roll of his eyes. "I've invited—no, commanded—my cousin Arthur's widow to leave London and come down to Cambridge. Monstrous woman. She's costing me a fortune in London. Must get her out of there before she beggars me entirely."

"Oh." Eleanor tried to ignore the sudden tightening in her stomach. The DeVaux family, all but Jordan, were a part of her life she very much wanted to forget.

"Never mind." He patted her arm, sensing her discomfort. "You will never have cause to meet her. Nor will I, if I have any say in it," he added with a grimace. "She'll live with my sister."

"Very well." Eleanor gave him a weak smile. "I'll go to the lecture. I've so enjoyed getting out more."

"Good." He clapped her on the shoulder. "I'm glad you go about. You were getting far too serious here. In fact—" He looked as though he was going to say something, then thought better of it.

"In fact what?" she prodded.

"Well, I was going to say that ever since you went to the Easter Term Ball with Caldwell, you've seemed different. More ready to be seen in society. I know it was a disaster. Lord knows what he was thinking, bringing you there. But at least some good came of it."

"Well"—she lifted her shoulders—"It was a night

of epiphanies. I realized I cannot continue to live my life in fear of what others might think of me."

DeVaux's brows rose. "Excellent. And high time. I'm only sorry your resolution had to spring from such an unpleasant experience. I wanted to draw Caldwell's claret for not realizing people would know you." He shook his head. "He sends his regards, by the way."

"Does he?" It was a matter of supreme indifference to her.

"Well, it wasn't in so many words. He just asked how you were. I'm sure he would have sent his regards if he'd thought about it."

Which of course he hadn't. The man lacked even a modicum of manners.

"He's been very distracted of late," DeVaux went on. "In a bear of a mood. I daresay it's because the Master has been hounding him. It sticks in Caldwell's craw that the man is always lording his social status over him. And the Master hates the fact that a man of no background like Caldwell can be such a resounding academic success."

Eleanor looked away, pressing her cold hands to her suddenly warm cheeks. "Has he been successful then?" she asked, completely unconcerned as to whether he was or not.

"Generally Caldwell seems to accomplish things effortlessly," DeVaux went on, irritatingly oblivious to the fact that she really had no interest in discussing his friend. "It makes the Master wild that he could spend the day amusing himself, out with the students, doing as he pleased, then spend all night at the observatory taking measurements and writing. It seemed he led a charmed life. Success in academics seemed to come quite naturally to him. But now—"

"Now?"

"Well, it's just that now he's working like a mad-man. Perhaps because he's had a flash of inspiration. Perhaps just to please the Master, though I doubt it. But he avoids everyone in favor of working. Even me. Actually, particularly me."

She wondered suddenly if Caldwell had heard the rumors.

She dropped her voice to ensure that the ladies did not overhear. "Jordan, you are not obliged to own William's paternity, you know. It does not miti-gate my crime and only drags you down with me. Just think of the harm it could do you at the university. Particularly now that you have family coming to Cambridge."

"No," he said sternly. "If there is anything I would ask for the sake of our long friendship it's that you do not deny it. As you say, it matters more to my rep-utation than yours if I choose to acknowledge Will as my own. Please respect that choice."

She looked at him for a moment, then opened her hands in a gesture of defeat. "I owe you every-thing. My life, even. But—"

"Arthur's widow is the one person who must never know about Will," he said tightly.

"Why—"

"I detest Phoebe DeVaux, but she must never know."

There was nothing to be done. She bowed her head. Likely it was folly to think Caldwell would have cared whether DeVaux or anyone else was her protector. She'd just been a temporary amusement for Caldwell, and now he'd moved on to other, more intellectual pursuits. She gave DeVaux a brief nod, led him back toward the circle of women, and, finding herself in urgent need of that genteel Eng-lishwoman's panacea, rang for more tea.

Chapter Eleven

Caldwell strode up the hill in a singularly foul mood. Actually, he'd been in a singularly foul mood the last few weeks. It didn't help that the spring duty of administering exams had had to be done under the eagle eye of the Master. It was a marvel that the man had so much spare time that he could spend it lurking around every corner waiting for the slightest wrong move on the part of the college fellows. The man had insinuated more than once that after the scene at the Easter Term Ball, Caldwell was but a hairsbreadth from being dismissed from Trinity.

It was enough to drive a man distracted.

And of course while Caldwell didn't mind stepping in to lecture in DeVaux's place, since DeVaux's cousin's wife had chosen tonight to make a dramatic entrance during dinner in the dining hall, he was irked—irrationally so—to find that the lecture on the classical origin of constellations was sited on his favorite hilltop.

Of course he could not claim it as his own, but it still improved his mood none to find his favorite private place swarming with fashionable members of the Cambridge Classics Society.

It was dark by the time he arrived. There were

perhaps twenty blankets and table linens set out on the hill. Everyone had brought a picnic feast, and the air hummed like a swarm of insects with low conversation. It was late March, by no means the best season for night picnicking, but everyone had wrapped up warmly and seemed rather unreasonably eager to hear about the adventures of the gods in the sky.

He felt a bit like an actor, or an animal on display in a menagerie. These richly gowned ladies in their fur-lined coats and well-born gentlemen gnawing the remains of cold game hen and asparagus saw him as a kind of amusement. Here he was, performing like a monkey for the gentry when he should be spending his time on his research.

He could not help but quirk a smile at their expectant faces. Truth to be told, it might be a rather novel and pleasant experience to lecture before an interested audience rather than distracted university boys pale from hangovers and debauchery.

"Greek gods were forever throwing people into the sky," he began. "Zeus and his wife, Hera, were particularly partial to it. Though it isn't very clear why they chose that mode of expressing themselves. It appears sometimes it was for punishment, sometimes for reward, sometimes merely to tell a story."

He shoved his hands into his breeches pockets, glad that he could indulge in this rather lowbrow habit while everyone's face was turned toward the night sky. "If you look there in the northern sky, you will see a set of stars in the shape of the letter W. That is Queen Cassiopeia, represented by her crown. She went about saying that her daughter Andromeda was more beautiful than the sea nymphs.

"Poseidon, father of the sea nymphs, was understandably piqued, and he told Cassiopeia that he would destroy her city in a tidal wave if she did not sacrifice the beautiful Andromeda to the sea monster Cetus. Here," he pointed, "next to Cassiopeia, is Andromeda chained to a rock, awaiting the sea monster."

He rather wished he'd brought his star charts. It was difficult to point out stars to people, particularly when the constellations never did look like what they were supposed to be. The Greeks had had quite an imagination. Too romantic by half.

"But fortunately for Andromeda, who should come along, in the nick of time, but Perseus? You can see him there, with his sword raised above his head, and that bright star representing the head of Medusa under his arm. Perseus petrified the monster with Medusa's head and married Andromeda, and they were all commemorated in the sky. Poor Cassiopeia over there is condemned for her pride to eternally circle the sky upside down."

He looked out over the twinkling land-constellation of dark lanterns that covered the hilltop. Every head was obediently tilted back, every chin to the sky. Except one insolent pair of eyes that looked straight into his. Eleanor's.

What the devil was she doing here? He hadn't thought she ever left Potton. He stammered through a few more legends, pointing out swans, dogs, and centaurs. "These collections of stars here, they represent the big bear and the little bear. Zeus, who was a bit of a philanderer, had fathered two boys by a mortal woman. When his jealous wife, Hera, found out, he turned them into bears and put them in the sky as protection."

"Why bears?" a woman asked. "That doesn't make any sense."

"Neither does hiding them in the sky, but that's how the legend goes." He rather wished he could find a place to hide himself. Eleanor was likely just as displeased as he was to find herself face to face with him. She'd made it quite clear during the silent carriage ride home after the disaster at the ball that she had no desire to see him again.

He cast her another glance, stumbled a bit, then carried on into a discussion of the meanings of the Greek zodiac, unwilling to let her know she'd rattled him.

The lecture seemed to last forever, though he had to give the Classics Society credit for their enthusiasm. Their questions outlasted even the trifles and pies in their capacious hampers.

At last he concluded and bowed slightly to the applause. Now to escape. He wished he had known Eleanor was going to be there. He wouldn't have come. And she of course had come expecting DeVaux. They would politely ignore each other and go their separate ways.

He slung his greatcoat over his shoulder and was preparing to make an undignified bolt for it when Lady Reed, indomitable leader of educational societies and lecture series, caught his arm.

"Is Professor DeVaux all right?" she asked. "He sent word at the very last minute that something unexpected had arisen. His letter seemed agitated."

"I assure you, madam, it was merely a family matter that needed his attention."

"Such a pity. But of course you were very gracious to lecture in his stead. I don't know when I've enjoyed a talk more. The society members are delighted."

"Thank you, madam."

Her hand tightened on his sleeve. "Do say you'll

lecture again. Several members of the Ladies' Literary Society have expressed a deep interest in your theories of the origin of stars."

"Certainly. I would be delighted. You were very kind to invite me." He bowed and turned to make his escape, but William caught him around the middle.

"Professor Caldwell," the boy exclaimed. "Where have you been? I finished my dam, and you never came to see it. And now I have all kinds of things in the garden coming up. Mama says we shall never be able to eat them all."

Caldwell could not resist the boy. "I'm sorry," he said, kneeling down. "I've neglected you shamefully. Did you finish the fort?"

He'd missed William. Missed his bright chatter, his intelligent mind. But as he listened, he caught himself scrutinizing the boy, looking for a resemblance to DeVaux. But at the moment all he could see were Eleanor's features in the sensitive brow, the well-formed mouth.

"Where is your mother?" he asked before he meant to.

"Here," she said quietly at his elbow. "Hello, Professor Caldwell. How have you been?"

"Well." He drew himself up rather stiffly. "I've been well."

"Good." She smiled.

"Good." Lord, he was standing staring at her like an idiot. The providential strike of a meteor would be the only thing that could save his self-respect. "Good," he said again.

He had to admit that the time away from his company seemed to have suited her. The small line of tension between her brows was relaxed. The perpetual look of anxiety in her eyes seemed stilled.

Heavens, she even wore a rather fetching shawl over her drab gown. Daring indeed.

"We've missed your visits."

He clenched his jaw to stop the groveling, mewling response that would have come out. "After our last meeting I believe it was clear that you preferred I stay away," he said at last.

She pressed her lips together and looked at the ground for a moment. "Perhaps the Easter Term Ball is best forgotten. I let my emotions run away with me. How foolish of me. William has suffered because of my stubbornness. May we begin again?" She held out a gloved hand to him.

He was reluctant to take it. Not because he did not wish to mend fences; after all, he was the one who had disappointed her, dragged her to that damn ball and left her to the wolves there. But to him she represented a temptation—one that would be forever out of reach. She was DeVaux's woman.

But he had no choice, so he gravely took her slender hand in his.

"Must you go?" she asked. "Or do you have time to walk for a moment?"

In response he held out his arm to her, and the three of them began a slow circle of the families packing up their dinners on the hilltop. Again he was struck by the change in her. He found himself wishing it didn't suit her so well. The thaw in her demeanor brought a new sensuality to the surface. Lucky dog, DeVaux. He'd better appreciate what he had.

They walked on, occasionally stopping to talk with Classics Society members. Eleanor seemed on easy terms with so many of them. Where was the ice queen? The woman who could freeze with a glance? Perhaps she saved it only for him.

Overall, it was less awkward than he had thought. Will was bubbling full of his projects and eager to get Caldwell's opinion. There was no chance for the awkward silences he was dreading.

"I was surprised to see you tonight," Eleanor said. "I had thought Jordan was speaking."

"He was. But his cousin's wife has arrived in town, and has proved to be more demanding than he anticipated. He asked me to do the lecture in his place. I'm surprised he didn't tell you," he added gruffly. Men should tell their mistresses these things.

Her expression, hard to see in the dark, remained neutral. "He hardly tells me everything. Particularly in matters to do with his family." She stopped and looked at him with an intent look on her face. "You know, we rarely see him. It isn't as though . . . that is . . . Well, he doesn't live in our pocket." She seemed, for a moment, inclined to say more, but she did not.

He found himself a bit cross talking about DeVaux. Everyone adored him. The Master, Will, Eleanor. And it had been a bit unfeeling of DeVaux to let him go panting after Eleanor when she was under his protection. Not that DeVaux knew, of course. And not that he'd really been panting.

He brushed the feelings aside. He should be glad this was cleared up. It kept things simple. After all, more time in her company and he might have grown to feel some ridiculous kind of partiality. And that was complicated.

"I'm glad it was you instead," she said unexpectedly. "I've been wanting to speak with you. I should not have spoken so harshly at the ball. I should not have let my own shame and vanity get in the way of our friendship."

Friendship. Yes, no reason they could not be friends. An odd pair they were, the knave and the queen. But he had to admit, he'd rather missed her conversation. When he'd teased her out of her reserve, she could be rather good fun.

Yes. Friends. And better to set things straight now with all the cards on the table. Nothing would get out of hand.

"You are looking well," he said, then wished he hadn't. Perhaps it sounded overly familiar. "I mean, you seem quite healthy. No, I mean happy. You seem happy." He looked up at the dark sky, praying for that meteor.

She smiled. "I am well. And it is thanks to you. You were right."

He looked down at her in amazement. "I was right? Good God, I must get that in writing. I'm afraid it rarely happens."

She did not laugh as he had meant her to. Instead she merely smiled and straightened the muffler that had threatened to part ways with Will. "No one cares about me or my past nearly as much as I had come to think. How very vain I have become." Her eyes were merry now, and it made her look quite young.

"Well, you hardly deserved such a cowardly escort to the Easter Term Ball." He said the words before he'd had the chance to consider them. "I should have stood up for you. That should teach you the lesson of going to social events with a man who is not of DeVaux's unimpeachable character."

She shook her head. "I realize now that you did not humiliate me on purpose. I also realize that I cannot live my life in fear of humiliation. Life is too short for that. And humiliation is self-inflicted."

"Well, you likely should have had DeVaux inflict

a few knocks as a lesson to me. But he knows I'm a rather dense fellow when it comes to social subtleties."

There was a silence. She looked at the sky for a long moment and then spoke. "So now that we are friends, perhaps you will call on me. On us, I mean, of course."

"Certainly." How could he possibly be friends with a woman so beautiful? He was going to go mad trying to resist pawing her like the ill-bred lout he was. "Perhaps William would like to go see the telescope tomorrow. Since he missed it before." Oh, trust him to bring up the embarrassing incident in the observatory. "DeVaux will be there," he added as an incentive.

Will grabbed her skirts and began pleading. She looked undecided for a moment, then relented. "As long as you don't let him touch any of your valuable instruments. And he shouldn't get overtired." The familiar, rather endearing look of motherly worry sprang up between her brows.

Strange how utterly dispassionate she could be about DeVaux. He was her lover, father of her child, for God's sake. And yet she treated him with no resentment, no warmth beyond friendship, none of the emotions he expected. Perhaps she truly had excised any formerly passionate part of her.

But he didn't really believe that anymore.

"I will bring him on the mail of course," she said. "There is no reason to send a carriage for us."

"Nonsense. DeVaux will loan his carriage. And you must stay for the fun. We'll show you the whole college. It's rather impressive, you know. And I can say without vanity that I know all the shocking secrets about it."

"Secrets?" Will echoed, suddenly as interested as Caldwell intended him to be.

"Oh yes, forgotten passageways, gory tales, murder, mayhem, treasures, everything." He shot Eleanor a look of devilment. She merely shook her head and rolled her eyes.

"Are you never serious?"

"Oh good Lord, never." He grinned. "But it does you good. You're such a terribly straight-laced, prim creature. If someone doesn't shake you up a bit, your face would set in that lovely haughty expression and crack."

"Here comes the accent," she moaned.

"The telescope will be grand to see, but I was really hoping we could go to the chemistry lab," William put in, leaping about the two of them like a cricket. "Do you think we could? Do you think they would show me how to make things explode?"

"William!" his mother said severely.

"I hear Jack Kittley makes a fine batch of gunpowder," John said, just to tease her.

They went on laughing and chatting just as though nothing had ever gone wrong between them. In some ways it was a comfort. And in most ways a torture.

He looked up at the sky and counted stars for a moment.

Good Lord but he wasn't cut out for this. He was a devil-may-care, pleasure-loving, rag-mannered bourgeois. Not some benevolent uncle or kind family friend. It wasn't as though Eleanor, or Will, actually *needed* him.

And, devil take it, he didn't want to be needed at all.

Chapter Twelve

"We really should go home," Eleanor said for the fourth time. But even she giggled, obviously realizing she sounded less convincing with each repetition. But they had spent such a marvelous afternoon laughing like lunatics over their failed attempts to fly a new kite of William's own design.

She leaned back against the oak log they'd finally chosen as the site for their belated picnic and offered Caldwell the last of the berries they had picked.

"Lord, no," he said with a groan. "Between your compulsive berry picking and Jenny's packed luncheon, I'm absolutely full to the gills."

"I'm going to explode," Will agreed cheerfully.

John had forgotten how appealing it was to spend a day in total idleness. And he had never seen Eleanor so merry. When she laughed it was genuine, all the way up to her clear gray eyes.

And now that she'd left off coddling him quite so much, Will was flourishing. He would always be more drawn to intellectual than athletic pursuits, but these days, after two weeks of vigorous outdoor play, he seemed more like, well, an ordinary boy.

Caldwell gave a relaxed yawn and wondered idly if he himself was as transformed.

"How are things at the university?" Eleanor asked. "You've devoted so much time recently to amusing William and me. Taking us to Swaffham Prior and the Devil's Dyke . . . I can't imagine when you have time to work. Does the Master not mind that you spend your afternoons gardening and picnicking and tromping about with us?"

He felt an unwelcome twang of guilt. The Master was always the fly in the ointment.

"There's really nothing I do that pleases the Master," he said, rolling his eyes. "To start with, I was born to the wrong family, was raised in the wrong neighborhood, keep the wrong company, and, of course, have the temerity not to give a hang what he thinks."

He pushed his hair off his forehead and half closed his eyes. If someone had told him two months ago that he would be wishing academic life to the devil and craving a life of bland, domestic pleasures, he would have choked on his ale.

Ah well, better put that analysis alongside his irritation with the Master and consign them both to perdition. For now, he was perfectly content to watch the lacy patterns of evening light and shadow shift across the grass and slide over the skirts of Eleanor's pale gray gown.

Rather too bad of Jordan not to have set her up in grander style. She was, after all, a lady, and it wasn't as though DeVaux couldn't afford it. Neglectful fellow.

Caldwell hadn't seen a hair of Jordan near Potton for weeks. Instead he was constantly dancing attendance on his late cousin's wife. Why, if Eleanor were under his own protection, he would find it well-nigh impossible to stay away.

Better, of course, that they were merely friends.

"You act as though your parents were beggars." She laughed her throaty laugh. "But I know it isn't so. And don't go trying to fob me off with some sad story of your charwoman mother and debtor's-prison father, because I know it isn't true."

He smiled up into the darkening sky. "Very well, the ordinary truth of it is that my parents were thoughtless enough not to die at a tragically young age. My mother is, very unfortunately, *not* a drunken washerwoman. And my father, despite what I might wish, has never murdered anyone with a mason's trowel for a farthing's worth of gin." He heaved a despondent sigh.

"Oh, I am sorry," she said dryly.

"I trust you will keep the secret of my shame when I tell you that my father is merely a solicitor in Cheapside, and my mother the sixth daughter of the younger son of a baronet. Hardly the thing novels are made of."

"I think it's rather better not to have a proper father," Will said sympathetically. "For then you can tell people anything you like. I told Tom Whitling and his brother that my father was a French spy and that he was hanged at Newgate."

Caldwell laughed at Eleanor's horrified expression. "You *are* lucky," he said. He watched Will go back to weaving a rope out of the long meadow grass and then settled down in an easy sprawl and allowed his head to fall back against the fallen tree trunk. Eleanor's shoulder was very close to his, far closer than DeVaux would approve, but DeVaux wasn't here, and he was too lazy, too comfortable, to move.

"Yes, I would far rather that my father have been a pirate and my mother the South American princess who murdered him with her poisoned hairpins," he went on. "But no such luck. I'm afraid my parents are excellent, sober people. They have a carriage and no fewer than two upstairs maids. Positively steeped in petit bourgeois respectability."

He grinned. "Very respectful of their betters, you know. The Master would be pleased to know that they are just as horrified by my life as he himself."

"Where are they now?" Will asked. He tested the strength of his grass rope and began idly binding one of his mother's pretty ankles to the remains of the kite.

"London," he replied. "Though not the area of London your mother knows. Needless to say, they were very distressed to have a son who showed signs of being academically inclined. Might give me notions of raising myself above my station. My father's a great believer in class structure. I believe he suspects I am a radical, ready to assassinate the king and spread liberty, equality, and fraternity through England." He made a comical face of resignation. "He and the Master would get along famously."

"They should be proud of your accomplishments," Eleanor said, frowning.

"Lord, no. It isn't the natural order of things. They're much happier with my sister, whom they married off to a respectable wool merchant. She'd caught the eye of any number of bucks of the town, but being of the lower gentry herself, my mother was dead against her daughter marrying into the ton. She knew they'd treat her scornfully because of her background. And she was very likely right."

"I hope at least that the marriage was a success," Eleanor said in a low voice. "Sometimes these arranged marriages can turn out quite happily."

"No," he replied in a brusque tone. "This did not. She would divorce him, or annul it—God knows the man is mad enough to warrant it—if she could, but of course it is not possible." He looked out over the lengthening shadows of the countryside in silence for a moment. "But my parents are pleased. After all, they have ensured a respectable alliance to which no one can object, and respectability is all."

"And were you expected to make a brilliant match?" she asked, smoothing her hands across her skirts. The leaf pattern of shadows gave the plain fabric the look of brocade. Caldwell himself was tempted to touch it as well; it looked so alluringly bright with gold. But of course he did not.

"Of course," he said, half closing his eyes to shut out the temptation. "I was expected to go into law, or perhaps the military. Marry someone plain who didn't spend too much money."

"A woman of character who is well educated, principled, industrious, moral . . . Goodness, what were all the things you said you required?" She shot him a wicked, almost flirtatious look.

"Indeed," he laughed rather sheepishly. How long ago that conversation seemed. Had he really said something so idiotic? "She must also play the accordion, smoke a good Dutch pipe, and know how to make a curry so hot it will blow my eyeballs out."

"Oh dear," she said mildly, though he could feel her shoulder shaking with laughter beside him. "I should not have wondered at your looking at me with such contempt when you met me. After all, we grand London ladies know nothing but how to spoil our lapdogs and think of new symptoms of boredom for our physicians to treat."

"Oh, I was a very rude fellow, wasn't I?" he said. "Though of course your ladyshipness didn't help.

Odd that my two favorite people would be high-born, don't you think? Stupid of me not to have realized you were together."

There. He could say it most naturally. And it was best to show he knew the lay of things.

"There is no liaison between DeVaux and me."

She said it so firmly that he could not help but turn and look at her. "Ah," he said at last, when he could think of nothing else.

"I know what people say," she went on, sounding almost angry, "but there is nothing between us."

For the first time in a long time, he really did feel out of his depth. Did the gentry really so cavalierly throw off their lovers and yet remain as close friends as she and DeVaux evidently were? He had rather thought Eleanor the one-love-forever type. Ridiculous of him.

"You've successfully evaded my earlier question," she said, turning the subject. "I asked you how things are at the university, and you instead give me a confession of your embarrassingly genteel back-ground. Your mother would be horrified by that dreadful accent you put on sometimes."

"You're just cross because you know you're not good enough for my family," he said mockingly. "You'll be combing the countryside for accordion lessons tomorrow, I'd warrant."

She was available then. Unattached. Whatever had been with DeVaux was over. He couldn't for-mulate proper thoughts.

"It would be hopeless," she sighed. "I could never live up to your strict standards of wifely accom-plishments."

He leaned back on his elbows and grinned at her. Better to be insolent than to fall into some horrify-ing sentimental talk. "I suppose you'll just have to pine away with love for me. I shall never unbend, you know. Except, perhaps, for the matter of the pipe. I'm not entirely unreasonable, of course. But on the matter of the curry I stand firm."

"Yes," she said serenely, "I suppose I will just have to be content to pine."

No liaison with DeVaux. The idea flew around his brain like a comet.

"Still no answer to my question about the university," she said with a frown. "It must be very bad indeed."

Will had now turned his kite into a kind of scarecrow with the grass rope wound into a ball for its head. Caldwell plucked a few creeping vines from the log and stuck them in the creature's head for hair.

"It's going terribly," he admitted at last. "I can't seem to do anything right. When I spend time with the students—tutor them, help them—I'm being overly familiar. When I leave them alone I'm neglecting them. My research is too academic and focuses on topics that cannot be understood by wealthy patrons who give us our endowments. God, how I envy DeVaux," he said with more feeling than he'd meant to.

But Eleanor was no longer with DeVaux. For all his handsomeness, cleverness, and breeding, she was no longer attached to him.

William lay his head in Eleanor's lap and looked up at the sky as it darkened to indigo. "There is a new moon tonight, right, Professor Caldwell? Can we stay until it's dark so we can watch the stars?"

"Oh, Will, it's been a long day. And your coat is not heavy enough," Eleanor protested.

"There will be meteors tonight," Caldwell said, almost to himself.

"Meteors? How do you know?" William demanded.

"The Lyrids always fall in April. And this year has been quite spectacular."

William stared intently at the darkening sky as though he expected a deluge of falling stars immediately.

"The meteors tonight are DeVaux's, you know," he went on, waving a hand at the sky. "He studies them. Likely he's up in the observatory right now, with his eye glued to the telescope. And meteors are beautiful, magical things. Easy to convince a patron to give more money for the study of meteors."

Eleanor made a sympathetic noise and looked up at the stars. Caldwell turned to face them as well. Truth to be told, he didn't envy DeVaux quite as much as he had a few moments ago.

"When one is so unfashionable and ornery as to study the formation of stars, people think, star formation? We have plenty of stars. Who cares how they got there? And why would we need more of them?" He laughed.

Her shoulder was so near to him that her sleeve brushed his cheek as she breathed. He sat upright and moved slightly away, just to ensure that he didn't end up with his own head in her lap like William. Apparently his body was determined that he should make a cake of himself.

"And DeVaux has the correct breeding and the correct manner of being friendly without letting one forget one's place," he went on. "I'm not the only one who maintains that DeVaux has it all. So don't think I'm complaining. He's fortunate to have a friend like me. I serve primarily to cast his perfection in higher relief."

She smiled, though she kept her face turned to-

ward the pale stars appearing in the sky. "Is that why
you envy him?" she asked. "Because the Master
fawns on him? Because his research is popular?
Surely not for his title. He only recently inherited
it, you know. A cousin died unexpectedly last year."

"Unexpectedly?" he snorted. "You could say that.
He died in a duel, I heard. Quite the bounder.
Fighting over some trollop, I expect. In fact, the
man's widow recently came to Cambridge. I've met
her, and she seems like good fun. Good riddance as
far as her husband goes, if you ask me. I went on a
boating expedition with her, DeVaux, and some of
the lads from the college not long ago."

"Oh." Her voice sounded strange in the darkness.
"How pleasant. Is she quite beautiful?"

"Yes," he said truthfully. He didn't think her as
beautiful as Eleanor, but that would sound odd said
aloud.

"I'm sure she makes a lovely curry," she said in a
tone that was almost pettish.

"Unfortunately, I doubt it." He looked up at the
sky. It was a clear night. Perfect. Normally on a
night like tonight he would be itching to go to the
observatory. But he found he was rather comfortable where he was.

With a satisfied sigh, he folded his arms behind
his head and squinted upward. His movement put
his right elbow just behind Eleanor's head, his
sleeve actually touching her bare hair. Not the
done thing, of course, but he was too lazy to move,
and she was too absorbed in stroking her son's
head in her lap to take any notice.

"Lady DeVaux is quite the society belle," he continued. "Though I suppose you were as well
before—well, before you moved to Potton. I rather
think you'd like her. She's not in the least bit grand.

And you know that is high praise from me. Shall I introduce you? Or DeVaux can, of course. After all, she's his cousin by marriage."

She was silent for a long moment, watching William's eyes grow heavy waiting for meteors.

"I don't believe Lady DeVaux would wish to meet me," she said at last. "In fact, if she knew I lived so close to Cambridge I believe she would be horrified."

"Why?" he demanded, insulted on her behalf.

"Because the man who killed *her* husband in the duel over a trollop was *my* husband."

He sat bolt upright and stared at her. "Good God," he breathed after a long pause. "Why doesn't anyone tell me these things?"

She gave a rueful laugh. "If you were more of a gossip, I daresay you would have known every detail long ago. It was well known, of course, even this far from London."

"Were you the trollop?" he asked bluntly.

She laughed genuinely this time. "I'm afraid not. Whitcombe and I had parted ways many years before. I never warranted such effort in my husband's estimation. And it wasn't Lady DeVaux either, as I can see you're wondering. She is entirely blameless, I assure you. By the time the duel happened last year, both men had long lost any interest in either of their wives.

"It was just some woman, too much drinking— the usual causes." She looked up at the sky. "Will there really be meteors?" she asked with forced cheer. "Or was this merely another way of forestalling the end of a lovely day?"

"And your husband was killed in the duel as well?" he asked. "I thought you said he died on the Continent."

"No. He wasn't killed then. He fled to Brussels, where he died not long after."

Caldwell wasn't certain what to say. Such wrenching dramas evidently did not befall the respectable sons of solicitors. He could have asked her a thousand questions: Did she miss her husband? Why had they separated? Did Whitcombe know that Will was not his son? But everything he wanted to ask seemed too intensely personal.

"There," he said suddenly. "Did you see it? A streak across the sky. It was gone in an instant."

Eleanor's chin jerked up, and she searched the heavens. "No," she said, disappointed. "I didn't."

She leaned farther back against the log and craned her neck. It looked so perfectly white in the darkness, he had to resist the urge to caress it.

"I'm not even certain what I'm looking for," she said. "I saw falling stars when I was a girl, but perhaps they are things like fairies, that only the young, innocent, and very hopeful can see."

"I'm none of those things, as you well know," he replied. "It requires only patience."

Didn't she know that being alone here in the dark with him was dangerous? With the comforting evening noises of the meadow around them and the rich blanket of stars above them, it was asking a great deal for him to resist her. But, he reminded himself, she'd proved quite capable of resisting his gauche advances in the observatory.

Just because her romance with DeVaux was over did not mean she would welcome anything more than friendship from him.

"There!" she said triumphantly. "I saw one. They're so quick." They watched in silence, waiting for a sudden white streak across an inch of sky. Every time one appeared she exclaimed in surprised pleasure, like a child at her first pantomime. The firmament was in good form tonight. He'd never seen the Lyrids so spectacular.

"So many?" she breathed. "Is it really supposed to happen?"

He leaned back on his elbows against the log. "It has happened every April since the beginning of time," he said with a laugh.

"I have missed so much until now," she murmured.

"Did you love your husband?"

She turned to him, surprised, but oddly not insulted, at his impertinent question.

"No," she said. "Ours was not a marriage based on love."

"Then I am glad you are free of him. Just as I am glad that Lady DeVaux is free of her husband. How the world must be full of long-suffering couples. If only all men like your husband and hers would be so considerate as to kill each other off."

She shook her head, her attention on the shower of sparks above them. Strange how it was easier to talk about things so intimate when they did not have to look at each other. "It isn't true," she said. "Lady DeVaux and I were unlucky. And your sister too. But that doesn't mean that there are no real alliances of love and friendship to be made."

He kept his eyes on the sky. "You are still an optimist."

"Just like a fireworks display," she murmured. "Only so silent. I must wake Will . . . in a moment." For a long time she said nothing while the meteors skipped and skidded across the sky. "No, I am not an optimist," she said at last. "An optimist spends her time in hope. I am practical."

"You no longer hope?"

"I no longer wait," she replied firmly. "I spent too much of my time in regret, in shame. I let too many things just happen to me. They were not really choices, not really decisions."

There were two brilliant meteors, one after another, right by Canis Major. He was pleased to hear her gasp of awe. Just as though he'd arranged this show for her. Ridiculous. "And now?" he prompted.

"Now I am different. I don't want to live by rules anymore. I'm certain I will continue to scandalize everyone. But it will be because I have decided to."

"Bravo," he said. "I approve of scandalousness. And what is to be your first shocking act? A chip bonnet before Easter? A dinner party without turtle soup?"

"You're horrid," she said in a low voice filled with laughter.

"I am," he agreed readily. He turned to her and found her looking directly at him, her clear eyes distractingly locked with his. "But you must give me credit for living according to your new creed," he said. "I do precisely as I please, damn the consequences. And see how happy I am?"

She thought for a moment, unreadable expressions moving across her face like clouds. "Yes," she murmured at last, as if talking to herself. "Damn the consequences."

And with that, she leaned in and kissed him.

He didn't expect it. He wasn't prepared. By the time his mind had caught up with his body, he had already tangled his fingers into her hair and pulled her into a deeper embrace.

She was bold, demanding—her mouth lush and sensual against his.

"You shouldn't," he said, giving her one last fair warning.

He could feel her pulse, light and fast behind her ear. He had not invented it in his mind; she felt it too—the burning promise that had always been between them. He pressed his lips to the tender skin where a vein throbbed behind the curve of her jaw.

"I know," she whispered. "But I am."

He was a drowning man. A man happy to go under the deep warm waters and never come up again. He realized instantly as her lips moved under his that he was far, far outside his realm of experience. She knew how to press against him; he found somehow that his mouth had opened slightly and her tongue had found his. He responded by deepening the kiss even more and heard her inhale in pleasure.

"Please—I—"

He could feel her woolen gown slide across the ribs of her stays as his hand moved lower, almost of its own accord. Good Lord.

Then with Herculean strength he pulled himself away. "Please what?" he said, looking straight into the erotic depths of those gray eyes. "Please no? Or please yes?"

Her lips parted, and she drew a shallow breath. Devil take it, this couldn't go on, her son was asleep beside them. But when would she ever be possessed with this sweet madness again? His arms tightened of their own accord, and he pulled her closer into another dizzying kiss.

"Eleanor," he gasped at last. God, his hands were roving over her body with all the finesse of a frenzied undergraduate with his first doxy. "I've thought of you so often." Thank heavens she kissed him again before he said all manner of ridiculous things.

"Don't speak," she whispered urgently. "Don't

think." Her fingers tightened in his hair, and she arched her slender body closer to him.

He couldn't think. Not if he wanted to. In a moment he would be blabbing about love or marriage or some such rot. He was half incoherent as he kissed down her throat to the neck of that prim gown. "I want you, Eleanor. I'll take care of you. Be mine."

"No," she whispered. Then, as though to soften her refusal, she turned his face to hers and kissed him gently on the mouth. The expression in her eyes was almost sad. "I will not. I will not be anyone's."

He wasn't exactly sure what he'd offered her. A role as his mistress? Love? Marriage? It didn't matter. She'd refused him.

He pulled back with a smile that was not entirely steady. "Of course not. I understand. I didn't mean to offend you." In his fervor, he must have sprained his chest muscles in some way. He felt an unexpected ache.

"You didn't offend me," she said with an inscrutable shrug. "After all, I started it. Though you were quite accommodating." She gave him a little smile. "I have only just found my independence. I cannot give it away so quickly. I have only just started living again." She touched his cheek in an unexpectedly tender gesture that made the ache in his chest swell. "But thank you for that. It's been a long time since I was kissed. And I can't bring myself to regret it at all."

He stared at her, utterly at a loss for words.

"I'll wake our chaperon," Eleanor said at last. "He would be so cross to miss the falling stars."

Chapter Thirteen

Eleanor awoke with a twist of dread in her stomach. Before she was even fully conscious, she knew what was happening. In the little room next to hers, she could hear the uneven rattling breathing of her son. She swung her legs out of bed and reached for the little flint and tinderbox, her heart pounding hard to keep up with her racing mind.

When she walked into Will's room, the light of her candle showed the tumbled bedclothes and the shine of the boy's open eyes.

"I didn't want to wake you," he said in a small, hoarse voice.

She tried to appear calm, but she could see her own hand shaking as she put it to his forehead. Mercy, but he was burning up.

This was her fault. She shouldn't have let him stay out in the night air to see the meteor shower. She should have paid attention and not let him get overtired yesterday. She should have made him wear a heavier coat. Instead she'd sat in the grass forcing John Caldwell to kiss her. So selfish. So thoughtless.

"It's just a bit of a cold," she said briskly, though of course they both knew it was far more serious. "I'll make a mustard plaster. Jenny will be up in a moment to help you change your nightshirt. You're soaked. Now just lie quietly."

She charged down the stairs, desperate to do something—anything—to help him, but knowing that once the inflammation had taken hold, there was little to do but make him comfortable and wait.

She woke Jenny and sent the sleepy girl to him while she herself assembled all the ingredients for the plaster. Oh, but she'd grown to hate that smell. As a child she'd always found its pungency comforting. A warm, spicy reminder that dear Nanny would make everything better. Now, its burn in her nose only brought back memories of so many other nights of impotent ministrations.

While the plaster heated, she slipped into the hall. Four o'clock by the white-faced clock ticking out solemn time on the landing. The doctor would not take too kindly to being dragged from his bed. Perhaps things were not so bad as they seemed at first. She was coming fully awake now and felt a bit calmer. Perhaps it really was only a cold. Perhaps she was overreacting.

She went back to stir the concoction. How stupid that she would suddenly wish to send a message to Caldwell. What could he possibly do? Comfort her? Tell her everything would be all right? Comfort was a luxury, and now she must be practical.

Even in the poky little kitchen she could hear the clock on the stairs clicking away. Wretched thing. It seemed so ominous. She hurriedly finished up. Upstairs, Jenny had lit a few more candles, but still the room seemed full of dark, stretched shadows.

"How are you feeling?"

William looked up at her with heavy eyes. "All right," he said. He didn't sound convincing. His breath was so loud and labored, it was like another presence in the room. Eleanor found herself gasping for breath along with him.

She made the boy drink some tea, bathed his face and hands, and applied the mustard plaster to his chest.

Will wrinkled his nose but said nothing.

"Shall I send for the doctor, ma'am?" Jenny asked from where she was making up the fire.

"Not yet. We'll wait for morning. Goodness, but the fire feels good. I hadn't realized it was so cold in the night. I shall have to buy more firewood in the village. Though of course, it is likely to warm up soon. Spring is always so unpredictable."

She chattered away, her cheerfulness likely more frightening than reassuring. But Will, sunk in lethargy, made no complaint, and Jenny slipped out of the room as soon as she was able. Still, long after it was obvious that no one was listening, she kept up a bright monologue. Anything was better than the silence around William's harsh breathing.

Morning came slowly; the sky was a full dome of flat gray, darker slightly in the west. Rain scratched fitfully at the windows. Will's eyes were closed, but his sleep was tarnished with feverish dreams from which he would often awake with a start.

She tried not to let it frighten her. After all, the boy had been ill before. But she had never before felt so directly responsible.

She sat at the small desk beside Will's bed, turning over and over the two letters she had written. One was a message to the doctor, explaining the situation and asking him to come as quickly as possible. The other was directed to Caldwell.

She put the second letter down, face down on the desk. No. She wouldn't send it. It was silly to bother him, particularly when there was a chance that this was nothing. There was nothing he could do, and it was better that Will be kept as quiet as possible. There would be time enough to contact Caldwell if she had news. She tried not to think of the kind of news she would need to tell him.

William broke into another spasm of coughing. This one was long and exhausted him long before he was done. She tapped the doctor's letter against the edge of the desk, biting her lip.

"When I cough," Will panted, "I see . . . stars . . . like . . . like Professor Caldwell's meteors."

Enough. She went to the door and found Jenny coming up the stairs. "Find someone in the village who can deliver this to Dr. Wyeth," she said quickly. "Dr. Stalk won't come, so it will have to be him. There's money in my reticule in my room." She shut the door, not feeling as relieved as she thought she would. Then, before she could change her mind, she snatched the second letter off the desk. "Wait." She emerged from the room as Jenny came out of the bedroom with her reticule. "Ask the messenger to deliver this one as well."

"Caldwell." The Master's jerky stride tapped down the hall. "Ah, I see you are here at last."

John looked up from where he and Jack Kittley had been painfully going over some physics principles. Damn. What now? He got to his feet. "Sir?"

"You've been spending precious little time here, haven't you?" The man looked around Caldwell's spartan chambers in disgust. "Slacking off a bit. Perhaps you feel that since your last publication was so well received you no longer have to put yourself to any effort."

"That isn't the case, sir."

"Perhaps you feel that, as the son of a Cheapside solicitor, your lectures will simply roll off your tongue without the least bit of study or effort."

"I had no intention of giving that impression," he said stiffly, feeling his cravat go tight with repressed rage.

"And then, two weeks ago, instead of applying yourself to your research, you gave a lecture for that vulgar Lady Reed's Classics Society. You didn't feel it necessary to ask my permission, I gather?"

"I'm afraid Professor DeVaux could not attend, so he asked me to speak in his place."

"DeVaux." The man rolled his eyes. "He's been as much trouble as you are. The two of you going off on a boating expedition with some students and DeVaux's widowed cousin, whoever she is. Not at all the thing. Makes the students too familiar. And now this lecture. Apparently you don't have enough official duties, Professor?"

Caldwell clamped his teeth together over a sharp retort. "I have a great many things to do," he said at last.

"Then I would suggest you spend a bit more time actually doing them." The Master's narrow nostrils extended in a sniff. "I have nothing against Lady Reed and her dabblings with the Classics Society and the Ladies' Literary Society. Many are fine people. But I fear Lady Reed suffers from the same lack of judgment as you. Rather too inclined to allow unsavory sorts into inappropriate venues." He allowed himself a thin smile. "In fact, I believe the, hem, lady, you so misguidedly escorted to the Trinity Easter Term Ball was there."

"You keep very close watch on such extracurricular activities," Caldwell said dryly.

The man gave a stiff bow. "I must. The reputation

of Trinity College is in my hands. Anything negatively
attached to you or your activities reflects badly on the
college. Now, Professor, since you apparently have so
little to do, I know you will be pleased to take on ad-
ditional responsibilities for Professor DeVaux while
he's away. Particularly as you are such good friends."

"Away?" Caldwell echoed. He hadn't heard about
that.

"He was called away unexpectedly this afternoon.
A family emergency of some sort."

"Of course I will lecture for him."

"Excellent. And I believe all Professor DeVaux's
students will need tutoring for the next few days.
And there is the matter, of course, of the article you
are writing for publication. I do hope you realize
that personal research and publication of that work
are important parts of your role here. We don't
have benefactors if you don't have discoveries."

Caldwell forced a smile. "Of course."

"Your lamentable tendency to associate with the
wrong sort of people must be curbed," the Master
said curtly. "Now"—he gave a sharp look to where
Mad Jack Kittley was attempting to slip silently from
the room—"you may continue with Mr. Kittley's lesson."

Caldwell bowed the man out of the room, the irritation thick in his throat. Taken to task again. He
should be used to it by now.

He had to admit he was rather annoyed with Jordan for leaving just now. He didn't have time to
take on DeVaux's duties on top of his own. It was
his own fault. He shouldn't have been spending so
much time with Eleanor and Will.

He had piles of work to do, lectures to prepare,
tutorials to teach. For the last week he'd eaten a
hasty supper while standing up at the telescope. He

looked around the teetering piles of books and papers on the desk. Devil take it, there was a pile of letters he hadn't even managed to open, never mind read. Three more had arrived yesterday.

"All right." He turned to Kittley. "Let's begin again."

They limped through the lesson together, Kittley as anxious as he was to get it over with. Caldwell felt the avalanche of things to do piling up in his head. When the boy dashed away at last, he grabbed a piece of bread, a slice of cheese, and a pile of books and quickly made his way up the road to the St. John's observatory.

It was raining hard and blustery, which suited his ill temper perfectly. With DeVaux gone, there was no one with whom he could vent his annoyance. No one who would roll his eyes and insist that there was no reason to fear he would lose his position at the university.

For the first time since he had come to Cambridge, he felt, well, he felt rather alone. Very well, nothing that a bit of work wouldn't cure.

Of course the weather had wrecked his plans to take measurements this evening, but he could still work out some calculations. He opened the door at the top of the stairs and drew a deep breath. The observatory was always calming.

Strange how, despite the hundreds of nights he had spent here, he could recall only one. Here is where she stood. Here is where Will slept. This is where he had so very nearly kissed her.

And then, just the night before last, under those spectacular Lyrids . . .

He brushed aside those thoughts. Daydreams of Eleanor would have to wait. Wait forever, if he knew what was good for him. Whatever it was that he had offered, she'd refused.

He'd been idle for too long. He dropped the books on the table and sat down. There was a letter caught between two of the books, so he pulled it out. Hellfire. He should have dealt with this correspondence days ago.

From his sister in London, most likely. Hardly likely to cheer him up, really. But perhaps it would remind him that he was not the only unhappy person in the world.

But the letter didn't bear a London mark, and as he smoothed it he saw that it was not, indeed, Susan's hand. Curious, he broke the seal and looked at the signature. Eleanor Whitcombe. What the devil?

It was a brief letter, only a few lines. And even when he'd read them over several times he wasn't certain he understood their meaning.

William is quite ill. I have sent for the doctor, but I fear for him. Forgive me for writing, but I thought you would wish to know.

William was ill? How ill? Eleanor always seemed prone to considering every sniffle a harbinger of death. Did she want him to come? Why didn't she say so?

If she'd sent for the doctor, the man was there by now, and there was certainly nothing he himself could do. Perhaps she wouldn't want visitors at a time like this. He looked at his pocket watch.

Blast and damnation, it had been more than twenty-four hours since she'd sent it. What was he to do now? Call upon her in the middle of the night? He felt his lungs collapsing in panic. How badly off could the boy be?

He took a breath and reminded himself that he was not in a position to take care of her as he might like. She was a dear friend. Nothing more. Galloping to Potton at this time of night would likely draw unwanted attention to her, which was the last thing she wanted. He was just a friend. He must do only what a friend might do, nothing more.

She'd said the night he'd kissed her that she wanted nothing more.

He dashed off a note of his own expressing wishes for Will's recovery and a request that she allow him to visit tomorrow. Yes, that was right. Calm and sensible. No need to get hysterical just because of her dramatic letter. The effect of calm was only somewhat destroyed by his scrawling handwriting and the spatters of ink. No matter.

He tore down the stairs and splashed across the court to demand that the porter find someone to deliver it. Why hadn't he opened her letter earlier? If she'd only indicated that it was urgent. Had it been delivered express or come by penny post? He couldn't recall.

He stood at the porter's lodge, ready to dash his brains out on the stone wall. Surely this was the right thing to do. He wondered if he could convince Stalk to go to the boy. He knew Eleanor would never ask him.

He heard the messenger's horse start off down the Barton Road and shouted at him that he'd give him an extra crown when he was back if he accomplished the fifteen miles in under an hour.

Likely the boy had had nothing but a cold and was already recovered. She really did coddle him too much. Likely she didn't want him hanging over her and the boy at all.

Then he stood in the rain and watched the clouds play over stars above Potton and wondered if he'd done the right thing.

Chapter Fourteen

Caldwell showed up at the door, fresh as May, with a bouquet of pink spring flowers. She had promised herself that when she saw him again, she would be calm and friendly, just as though nothing had happened. She would not berate him for not coming to Will's bedside sooner. She'd obviously misjudged their relationship for expecting it.

"How thoughtful of you to come to inquire about Will," she said. He looked so brushed and neat. And as always, so wretchedly handsome. She smoothed a wrinkle out of her gown and forced herself not to tidy her unkempt hair.

"You look tired," he said. "But DeVaux said the boy was mending. Is that true?"

How stupid of her to have thought he would race to be at her side. If only for Will's sake . . . She turned away and handed the flowers to Jenny and ordered tea.

"Yes, he is better," she said. "The doctor is with him now."

John did not take the seat she offered him but turned to pace the room. "Was he very ill then?"

She drew a breath. It was difficult to recall those long fear-burnt days without pain. "He was. We feared for his life."

The man actually had the audacity to look surprised. "Well, why didn't you tell me that, Eleanor? Your note was so cryptic. I would have come immediately."

She resisted the powerful urge to stand up and break the vase, now filled with his flowers, over his head. After all the agonies she'd suffered over writing to him, he hadn't come. "I am sorry if the magnitude of his illness wasn't clear. I daresay you thought I was exaggerating," she said through her teeth.

There was the faint, nervous sound of a man clearing his throat, and she looked up to see the doctor poking his nose around the doorframe. "Come in, sir," she said, rather relieved to have another presence in the room. "How do you find him today?"

The very young man smiled a bit breathlessly and shifted his weight between his feet. "I believe William is improved, madam. At least, he seems so. I bled him a bit, and he rests more quietly now. I've left some more laudanum as well."

"Are you certain it is good to bleed him so often?" She could not help but ask. "He seems so weak."

"We must," he said, looking rather anxious. "His blood is tainted, and that is what makes him cough so." He pulled out a black book from his pocket and consulted it. "Indeed. The book says . . . that is . . . well, at least . . . anyway. I'll be back tomorrow."

"That's the doctor?" Caldwell asked scornfully once the man had taken his leave. "He's a child. Barely done with his training. And a fool to boot. Honestly, Eleanor, could you not find someone more experienced?"

She drew herself up. "Dr. Wyeth is Potton's doctor," she said coldly. "And I'm afraid Dr. Stalk has made himself unavailable to us."

"Because you wouldn't give yourself to him," he said darkly.

"Are you saying I should have?"

"Of course not. I'm just wondering why you didn't go to someone more experienced than that greenhorn."

She clenched the handle of her teacup very tightly for a moment. "I did the best I could. Under the circumstances."

She was glad he looked wounded. But really it was her fault. She should not have expected him to come. Particularly when the last time they'd met she'd turned down his offer of a closer liaison. She had no right to demand his support.

He ran a hand through his reddish brown hair. "I could have helped if I'd known. I should have read your letter when it arrived, but I—well, it doesn't matter. I let you down unforgivably." He jerked his waistcoat into place with an impatient gesture. "Dash it all, why does this have to be so complicated?"

"He's asking for you, ma'am," Jenny called softly from the top of the stairs.

"Thank you for coming to see about Will," she said, annoyed to hear her voice tremble. "As you heard from the doctor and from DeVaux, he is recovering. Good day." And without even seeing him to the door she fled upstairs.

Will looked as white as the bandages on his poor thin arm. His eyes were closed over deep circles, but she could tell he was not asleep. His breath was loud in his throat. She kissed his cool forehead.

"How are you feeling?"

"All right." He opened his eyes and gave her a

weak smile. "Better, I suppose. Can we open a window?"

She hesitated. Dr. Stalk had insisted that sickrooms be close and hot as a furnace. She herself felt nearly faint from the airlessness.

"Please, Mama. I can't breathe. It's so stuffy."

She reluctantly went to open the window a crack. The spring air was so reviving and clean. She watched Will turn toward it and inhale. She sent up a little prayer that she hadn't signed his death warrant.

"Professor Caldwell!" Will exclaimed. "I've been hoping you would come see me."

Eleanor spun and saw Caldwell, bold creature, walk uninvited into the sickroom. His vaguely self-mocking expression transformed so quickly into one of alarmed concern that she wondered for a moment if he would flee in terror.

"Feel better?" he croaked, turning up a smile that looked strained.

"A bit," Will replied. "I've been so bored. Mama won't let me do anything."

Caldwell approached the bed and gingerly sat down on the chair beside it. "You do look as though you're quite tired," he said.

"Professor DeVaux came to see me," he said with pleasure. "I don't remember all of his visit. I was a bit tired. But Mama said he stayed up with me for two whole days."

A peculiar expression crossed Caldwell's face. "That was good of him. I know he cares for you a great deal."

He turned toward Eleanor. She had never seen him with such a sincere look of humility. She did not want to melt. She did not want to forgive him for everything just because he looked so very regretful. She dropped her gaze to the floor.

"Your letter, Eleanor," he said in a thick voice. "I didn't read it until last night. And even then I thought you might be exaggerating. Worrying unnecessarily. I would have come straightaway if I had known—"

"It doesn't matter," she said quietly. "When you didn't come I sent for DeVaux."

He looked as though she had slapped him. "I let you down."

It was better this way. She'd grown to lean on him too much. She'd started thinking Will was special to him. No, honestly, she'd begun to think that *she* was special to him.

She had turned him down, she reminded herself brutally. He'd offered more. But in her own pride she'd wanted independence. But independence had a rather lonely price.

"You have no obligation to us," she said stoutly. "And it was foolish of me to have written you in the first place. I would have done better to have written Dr. Stalk and begged him to come. After all, there was nothing you could have done."

He looked at her for a moment, then turned away. "Perhaps you'd like me to read to you?" he asked Will. "Let's see what you've been hearing. Oh dear. *Sermons for the Moral Improvement of Children.* That would blue-devil me, ill or not. Perhaps we can find something more exciting. After all, when your body is improving it seems rather hard to ask your mind to improve as well. You know, I have a rather interesting book on Barbary pirates at home. Perhaps I'll bring it tomorrow."

"You could tell me one of those star legends," Will suggested. "Like you were talking about the

night of the star lecture." The boy looked interested for the first time in days.

Caldwell obligingly launched into the Greek
myth of Orion. His voice was perfectly gauged to
the sickroom, comforting and quiet. She felt the
urge to curl up next to him and listen in. What
would it be like to lean her head against his chest
and hear those stories rolling out of him?

What an odd notion. She had never done such a
thing.

She gave herself a mental shake and slipped out
of the room. Outside the door she stood for a moment and tried to gather her thoughts. Nothing
had changed, so there was no need to feel as
though she'd been turned on her head. She should
be glad for a few minutes to herself. Will's illness
had meant that a thousand things had been left un-
done. Now was the time to weed the garden, make
the shopping list, order the faulty chimney in the
drawing room repaired, create a tempting dinner
for Will's meager appetite. When she walked into
the kitchen, she was surprised to see Lady Reed
coming up to the back door.

"There you are," the woman said, breezing in
without preamble. "Excellent. The boy is better? I
heard he was. He's a fighter, that one. Now don't
go making yourself ill in taking care of him. You're
worn to a shadow. Have you eaten anything decent
since he fell sick? I didn't think so. You're gaunt,
Eleanor. And pale." She pinched Eleanor's cheek
as though she were a child. "Now don't be ridiculous in putting the kettle on. You and I should not
stand on ceremony."

She herself put the kettle on and drew up a stool
for Eleanor. "Here, I'll tell you what—I'll make you
up a lovely bit of bread and butter. Now just sit

down and let me fuss—it's the only way to be rid of me, you know. And you need some ale. It will give you strength. No ale? Well, tea will have to do. I'll make it strong. You've no more sense than a kitten when it comes to your own health. I was just the same when my George had the measles."

Eleanor sat helplessly in a chair while Lady Reed bustled about her small kitchen. She must be more tired than she thought. Lord, she was near bursting into tears with gratitude.

Lady Reed graciously feigned not to notice. "Now dear, you eat and I'll talk. I just thought I'd drop in to see how your boy fared and to keep you up to date on the Literary Society.

"We missed you at the last meeting. Poor Miss Jennings was anxious to get your opinion on prison reform, and of course everyone sent their best wishes as to your child's recovery. DeVaux was here?"

To Eleanor's surprise, the woman had actually stopped to wait for an answer. She swallowed the bite of bread and butter. "Yes. He's been very good to us."

"Yes. He's a lovely man. Can be a bit stiff, but he's very good-hearted. I've known his family for ages. Now, Eleanor, there is something I would like to discuss with you." She narrowed her large brown eyes thoughtfully. "A young lady has come to Cambridge, and I would like to propose her for membership in the society."

"Indeed," Eleanor said, "you do not need my permission."

"Perhaps not. However, this woman is Arthur De-Vaux's widow."

A gulp of hot tea burned down Eleanor's throat. "Indeed."

"Now, London scandal does not often get down here, but if I recall correctly, it was your husband who killed hers in that duel last year."

"Yes," she said tightly. "It was."

"Now"—the woman tapped her fingertips together—"I don't exactly know the etiquette required in the situation, but I wanted to speak with you first."

She almost giggled. *Was* there a prescribed etiquette in such a situation? "I—I have never spoken with Lady DeVaux. My husband and I had parted ways many years before the—the event happened." She drew a breath. "I will certainly resign my membership to make things more comfortable for Lady DeVaux."

To her surprise Anabelle Reed laughed. "Nonsense. Unless I'm misinformed it was good riddance to both your husbands. I merely thought that you might wish to meet each other alone before you met with the society."

She nodded woodenly. Meet Lady DeVaux? They had never been introduced. What would she say? It was not as though she could offer an apology on behalf of her husband and expect that they would shake hands and be friends.

She pressed her head between her hands. This was not how she had planned her life. She'd intended to spend the rest of her days quietly in Potton. She saw that Lady Reed was still talking and nodded mindlessly to whatever she said.

How stupid that she should wish to go to Caldwell for advice. After all, he hated complications. He had made it abundantly clear that while he was happy to befriend them for picnics and outings, he had no interest in becoming embroiled in the farcical drama that surrounded her real life. Still, she would have given a great deal just to lean against his chest and listen to him tell a story. Just for a moment or two.

"You're not listening to me in the least," Anabelle said cheerfully. "So you'd better confide in me and get it over with."

Eleanor smiled. "There is nothing to confide, really. I was just thinking that not so long ago I was congratulating myself on having learned to make better decisions about my life. And now I find that I should not, perhaps, have been quite so confident."

Chapter Fifteen

William looked at himself in the mirror with an expression of loathing. "I look stupid," he complained, dragging at the collar of his best suit. "Why do I have to dress up? I never usually have to dress up when Professor DeVaux comes to visit."

"He's bringing his cousin, Lady Phoebe DeVaux, with him," Caldwell replied patiently, even though this was the fourth time they'd had this conversation.

Will rolled his eyes. "Well, it isn't fair. I've been ill. I shouldn't have to dress up."

Caldwell was rather relieved that the boy had recovered to the point that he could complain. The last weeks had been difficult, as the boy made halting progress. Eleanor, of course, had been correct. The boy's illness had not been trivial.

He'd been rather flattered to see how much William looked forward to his visits. And frankly, he looked forward to them himself.

Devil take the Master and his ominous glares. He hadn't missed a single lecture or a tutoring session. How he spent the rest of his time was none of the man's business. If he wanted to race hell for leather to Potton every day, that was his business.

He knew it was too little too late, but he had to

do *something*. Something to prove to Eleanor, and to himself, that he was not completely self-centered and irresponsible. Something to show that if he'd understood the circumstances, he would have been right at Will's side from the start.

It was a relief, after so many anxious days, to see Will making what promised to be a complete recovery.

"Is your mother nervous about meeting Lady DeVaux?" he asked, just by way of making conversation. After all, he wouldn't blame her if she was. Phoebe was a lovely woman, as unpretentious as Jordan despite her high breeding. But what would he feel in Eleanor's place? The circumstances were indeed . . . unusual.

The boy shrugged. "Don't know. She baked a lot. And cleaned a lot. I wish Lady DeVaux wasn't coming. I would much rather wear my normal clothes and read with you about Barbary pirates."

"She's been rather quiet of late," Caldwell said. That was putting a shine on it. Eleanor had been virtually silent. His clumsy attempts at explaining himself back into her good graces had all been stymied by her remote, slightly worried expression.

"I guess." Will gave another tug at his suit. "Come on. I want to wait downstairs for Professor DeVaux."

Caldwell followed the boy down the stairs. He'd made a muck of this. Eleanor needed someone to help with Will. There were no two ways about it. And the only way to ensure that for the future was to marry her. DeVaux obviously wasn't going to do it, and, well, dash it all, someone should.

Despite what she'd said the night of the meteor shower, that she would belong to no one, she must be persuaded to be practical. Even if she did not love him, surely she could see that marriage provided many benefits. For William's sake. And she was a practical woman, wasn't she?

Marriage to Eleanor Whitcombe. The idea wasn't nearly as odd as he'd thought it would be.

It was a simple and sensible solution to a great many issues. She would have stability, a modest income, a father for Will, and society's instant and hypocritical forgiveness for all her past transgressions. He would have . . . well, he would have *her*.

The idea had lodged in his head several weeks ago and had refused to be dismissed. He'd even surprised himself by going as far as mentioning his plan to DeVaux one morning in the senior combination room at Trinity. Considering DeVaux's past relationship with Eleanor and the fact that she was raising his son, DeVaux had been surprisingly amenable to the idea.

Perhaps there really was a difference between the gentry and ordinary people. Caldwell himself found it difficult to imagine how such a friendly but detached relationship had evolved between Jordan and Eleanor. Had their passion really been so short-lived? He didn't want to think of Eleanor as fickle.

Well, emotionless as they might be, he himself would benefit from it. It was obvious that DeVaux had no interest in being further involved in the Whitcombes' lives. And obvious, thank God, that Eleanor didn't mind.

He was glad Eleanor was practical. Practical was good. But if she married him, would she look at him the way she looked at DeVaux? A man she was perhaps fond of but did not love. He shook himself. Since when was he so concerned that she love him? Respect and admiration should be plenty in a marriage. And he was indeed determined to marry her.

However, Eleanor had proven to be surprisingly

resistant to a courtship that was composed entirely of slinking over to her house, disappearing into her son's sickroom, and reading to him for a few hours.

Blast it, she must be made to see the advantages of a match with him. He was hardly a brilliant catch, but he was offering, and there was no denying the physical attraction that had always simmered between them. He could give her her beloved independence, while still giving her the advantages of a respectable standing in the eyes of the world. That would tempt her? Surely?

He hadn't actually gotten up the courage to test this theory.

But today was the day. Today he would propose to her.

He went downstairs and found Eleanor standing in the hallway smoothing her hair as she looked in the small mirror hung on the wall. "DeVaux is bringing her?" she asked.

No need to ask who she meant. "Yes. I believe Boxty Fuller was to have accompanied her originally, but he was unable to come at the last minute. I said I would ride out to meet them. I am not certain DeVaux wishes to be alone with his cousin's wife."

Eleanor laughed, but it was strained. "Is she so terrible then?"

"Not in the least. You will like her a great deal."

She'd made an effort about her appearance. The modestly cut sprigged muslin gown she wore was not the first kick of fashion, but it looked well on her and was certainly an improvement over the drab things she usually wore. She looked nearly as uncomfortable as Will. He resisted the unexpectedly protective urge to grab her up and kiss her.

Out the window he could see that Will had

slipped outside and was already looking down the road for their visitors, switching a stick and happily rumpling his clothes.

"Lady Reed was just here. She often drops by to ask after Will," Eleanor said, turning anxiously to the mirror once again. "I should have introduced you, but I didn't want to interrupt you and Will." A pretty blush rose up her cheeks. "I believe I didn't wish her to know you were here. She is of course very open-minded and one of the kindest people in the world, but she is so very inclined to tease me." She gave a little smile.

"Well," he laughed, "I'm glad I didn't bumble downstairs demanding to know where you keep the towels."

She smiled. "Yes, call it cowardice, but I feel my reputation is too frail to withstand a single man not only in the house but upstairs. For all my grand proclamations that I don't care what people say, there is no need to shock everyone."

"Everyone knew DeVaux ran tame here," he said, realizing with horror that he sounded almost as jealous as he felt.

"That was different."

"Why?" he asked.

"It . . . it just was," she said irritably.

He continued down the last few steps and propped himself up on the occasional table in the hallway. "It was different because he was your lover, and I am merely your friend?" An idle question, of course. Just to see where the land lay.

She turned from the mirror at last. "No. No. Not that at all." She made a flustered gesture. "Quite the opposite. That is . . . well, it's just different, that's all. I know it doesn't make sense."

"Who cares what people think? We ourselves know that my visits are innocent."

"I know," she said. "And I don't give a rap for what is said. But . . ."

He picked up a small vase of flowers on the table and examined it as though he'd never seen anything like it. "Shall I stop coming by then?"

Her gaze flew to his. "No. I don't want you to stop. That is, Will and I both . . ."

He traced the pattern on the vase with his forefinger. "Perhaps if our friendship was made more respectable?" He let the words hang in the air and tried not to look as though he was holding his breath.

She cocked her head. "I don't understand." The clock began its grinding whir in preparation for striking. "Is that the time?" she exclaimed, launching into motion again. "Oh, they'll be here soon. Put down that vase—you're dripping water on the rug." She took it from him and pushed him down along the hallway as though he were William. "Heavens, what was I thinking, inviting that woman to visit? The drawing room chimney still doesn't draw right, and the settee needs new upholstery."

"She's not a monster," he said. "And the bad business was between your husbands. Not between yourselves."

She was grumbling her protests when he stopped and turned around.

"Eleanor," he said quickly, before he lost his courage. "I know things between us have been a bit strained. You've been worried about Will and of course this business with Lady DeVaux. But Will is better now, and I've been thinking a great deal. That is, I've been thinking a great deal about my position at the university and what I might have to offer . . . That is, after the night we watched the Lyrids when you said . . . that is—"

Jenny came barreling down the hall and nearly ran them down. "Ma'am, I wanted to get your instructions as to the tea. I'm afraid I could not find watercress this morning. I looked for ages, I did. And there isn't enough cucumber from the garden. Shall I run out for more? Do you think the lady will be asking for fancy biscuits? I only have the ordinary sort I make, but I could go to the baker in town if you don't think it's too late."

"Mama," Will called from the front door, "may I have a bit of cake before they come? I'm *starving*."

This was not the time to propose. It would have to wait. He caught Eleanor's chin and made her stand still for a moment. "I am going now to meet DeVaux and ride here with him and Lady DeVaux," he said. "The visit will go very smoothly, you'll see. And when she is gone, and when you are calm again, there is something I would like to speak with you about."

She nodded dumbly, likely as not completely unaware of what he'd said, and then turned and fled to the kitchen.

Eleanor felt as if she had spent seven lifetimes waiting for Lady DeVaux's carriage. Fortunately, Will appeared dirty kneed from trying to catch a frog at the side of the road, and she was able to while away a bit of time scolding and brushing and tidying.

Then all at once, there was the rumble of wheels and horses, and Lady DeVaux had arrived.

She went outside to greet them and was rather taken aback by the figure that stepped out of the carriage. The woman was elegant and quite beautiful, to be sure, but she had none of the proud bearing or scornful expression she had expected from Arthur DeVaux's wife.

She was glad Caldwell and Jordan had accompanied Lady DeVaux, but self-conscious too. Perhaps this meeting should have been arranged in strict privacy. What must the woman think of her? Should she mention the duel and apologize on her husband's behalf? Could one ever apologize for something so dreadful? Or should she pretend nothing had happened? Surely that wasn't right either.

She pushed down the sensation of panic and felt herself retreating behind her usual mask of reserve while they fumbled through introductions.

"Won't you come in and see Will?" she asked, once they seemed to have run out of banal comments. "He's much better. You'll be so pleased, Jordan. He asks for you every day and was in raptures to hear that you were back again so soon."

Caldwell made an odd noise in his throat, almost like a grumble, but this was not the time to ask what he meant by it.

Will, only slightly more disheveled than when she'd walked out a moment before, pounced on DeVaux immediately. Eleanor looked around the drawing room, feeling acutely self-conscious. It was such a drab little place. And the chimney wasn't working right at all. Lady DeVaux must think she had fallen very low indeed.

"There is someone I'd like you to meet," Jordan was saying to Will.

"Lady DeVaux," the boy replied with admirable politeness. "The wife of my father."

There was a horrified moment of silence.

Eleanor flashed a look at DeVaux. Surprisingly, he looked unmoved that her son had, within two seconds of meeting Lady DeVaux, divulged the very secret that Jordan had insisted it was imperative to keep from her.

"I thought it better that he should know from the beginning," she said weakly at last. What else could she do? Deny it?

Lady DeVaux neither screamed nor fainted. "Hello, William," she said with perfect aplomb, giving him her hand to shake. She looked as though she happened upon her husband's stray children every day of the week.

Eleanor moved to DeVaux's side. "Oh Jordan, I'm so sorry," she whispered. "You know I never kept Will's past a secret from him. I never thought to warn him—"

"She'd deduced it already," he said quietly. "I suppose she knew Arthur's character as well as anyone."

"And yours, to want to protect her from the truth," she retorted.

DeVaux shrugged in his usual way. "And of course, one look at the boy confirmed it."

Eleanor was suddenly very conscious of Caldwell's eyes upon her, accusing. Lord, he hadn't known either, of course. He'd thought, like the rest of the world, that Jordan was Will's father. This was getting complicated. And she knew how much Caldwell hated complications.

"Perhaps Lady DeVaux would like to see your garden," she suggested to Will, going back to rejoin the conversation. "I'll have the tea things set out on the lawn, and we will all take our tea there when you are finished." Mercy, between Caldwell's glares and the wretched chimney, the air in the room was barely breathable.

Happily, Lady DeVaux graciously accepted this suggestion and allowed Will to lead her out to the back garden.

"What do you think of her?" Jordan asked, following Eleanor into the kitchen and propping himself up against the wooden table in the middle of the room.

She looked out the back window to where Will was enthusiastically expounding on the merits of his vegetables. To her credit, Lady DeVaux actually looked interested.

She smiled. "She is beautiful, fashionable, and horribly, wretchedly likable," she pronounced.

"Indeed." He looked a little grim. "I'm afraid I'm not in her good graces at the moment. She discovered Will's existence when he fell ill. I told her he was my child, but it didn't take her long to figure out the truth."

"Nor should you be in her good graces," she said tartly. "You should have told her the truth from the beginning. Or at least as soon as she found out about William."

Caldwell made a noise very like a snort.

"I'm surprised she has been so gracious to me," she said, ignoring the man. Though the affair had taken place before Arthur had married Lady De-Vaux, the woman had every reason to hate her.

Indeed, Eleanor had been surprised by Phoebe DeVaux. She'd expected someone grand, cold, self-righteous. Or perhaps someone beautiful and stupid. Arthur would have tired of someone clever or serious. Instead Arthur's wife was warm and polite and showed every sign of good sense. Yes, wretchedly likable.

"She knows what Arthur was like, Eleanor," De-Vaux said darkly. "Charming. Inconstant. She does not blame you."

"Lord," said Caldwell in his best East London accent. "What things the gentry do get up to. I never knewd it was so tangled. As good as a play."

She shot him a frustrated look. Of course he was annoyed that she hadn't told him the truth before. And she'd wanted to. But Jordan had been so adamant that the secret be kept. "I'm glad my weakness of character and blackened reputation has served to amuse you, Professor Caldwell," she said dryly. "Now, if you will oblige me by carrying out the tea things?"

"So you like her?" DeVaux said again as they moved toward the back door.

She laughed. "Indeed I do. I hope she will come to us often. Lady Reed is determined to have her join the Literary Society, and Will looks fair besotted." She narrowed her eyes at him. "You seem very anxious that we like her. Why?"

"No reason," he snapped. "It is merely that I find her to be a bit quick-tempered and spoiled."

"Only because she is angry with you for keeping such a stupid secret," she retorted. Then she smiled. "I'm surprised you care if she is angry. It isn't like you to care what anyone thinks."

"I don't."

"He protesteth too much," Caldwell said mildly. He made a flippant gesture and picked up the tea tray, but Eleanor could see he was still wounded. Honestly, she was a bit surprised. Why did it matter who William's true father was? After all, she couldn't imagine that he was so puritanical that he would care about the sordid details when he already knew the crime.

"The secret was old and long past any keeping," she said. "It is better that everyone know the truth now."

"Well," Caldwell said, with the familiar mocking twist to his mouth, "neither of you has my support. Too much intrigue by half. I side entirely with Lady DeVaux."

Tea was accomplished with virtually no mishaps and only a few lapses in mild, pleasant conversation. Caldwell observed that the two ladies worked so hard at being convivial that he was obliged to step in with remarks on the weather only twice. DeVaux, however, spent most of the visit watching Lady DeVaux, his eyes alert, his expression wary. And Will, after eating as much cake as his mother allowed, was quite willing to fill any conversational lapses with questions to Lady DeVaux on the kind of horses she kept, the cake she preferred, and whether she thought the fort structurally sound enough to add another floor.

Once tea was done, Will, enthusiastic as always, suggested they walk down by the river to see his dam, and so they all obediently trooped through the meadow to the brook. DeVaux joined Lady DeVaux and William and left Eleanor to walk along with Caldwell in silence.

"It is a very fine day," she began, casting him a hopeful smile.

"Very fine."

"I hope you don't mind going to see the dam again. After all, you must have seen it half a dozen times by now. But Will is so proud of it."

"I have no objection to seeing it again," he replied. She seemed nervous in her awkward forays into conversation with him, but he was in no mood to help her.

Indeed, she had no reason to be nervous. Lady DeVaux had been perfectly amiable, and indeed, she and Will showed every sign of becoming thick as thieves. Jordan, his normal, taciturn self, had even exerted himself to be charming. The afternoon could be deemed a success.

Eleanor twisted the ribbons of her bonnet, retied the bow, then pulled it loose again. "I think it is all going well, don't you?"

"Certainly."

"It's too bad Will spilt tea all over himself, but she was very gracious about it."

"Of course."

She pressed her gloved hands together and walked in silence for a moment. "I understand if you're angry with me," she said.

"Why would I be angry? I have never pried into your past." She hadn't trusted him enough to tell him the truth. And he had felt such guilt about falling for Jordan's former mistress. Worried that Jordan would be offended. Worried that Eleanor still cared for her former love. He felt like such a fool.

"Of course you did," Eleanor retorted. "You were perfectly dreadful when you came calling on me that first time. I could have wrung your neck. But since then, no, you have never pried." She watched Will splash across several stones to the dam in the brook, obviously repressing her motherly warnings.

Caldwell felt as though he'd been relegated to a minor character in a play when he'd thought he'd had a leading role. He'd thought this was about Eleanor and him, with Jordan bowing out in the third act. But now, to find out there were other players he'd never even heard of? Some dead cousin who'd caused all the trouble? He'd been wrong. The story was about Arthur, Phoebe, Jordan, and Eleanor. He himself was merely a walk-on part. Man in scholar's gowns. Suitor number two.

"Where were you nine years ago?" Eleanor asked suddenly.

He stared at her in surprise. "Nine years ago?" He thought for a moment. "I had finished university, and I was working as a tutor in Essex. Why?"

"Then you know little of my history."

He shrugged. "I know more now." Even to himself he sounded petulant. "Eleanor, with you it's one mystery after another. Always so complicated. I don't care about your past. Jordan's child, Arthur's child—it makes very little difference to me."

"Yes, I'm sure it doesn't. But I wish to tell you anyway, if you will listen."

They had reached the edge of the river. It really was a lovely place, shady and pale green with new spring grass. There were tiny pink and white wildflowers growing up along the muddy banks, and the snow thaw had provided enough water to make the little brook babble in an entirely respectable manner.

Behind Will's spillway, the water had backed up into a large pool. It was picturesque, though rather murky, and of course served no purpose at all. Will had rather grand plans of stocking the pool with frogs and fish, but at the moment, it looked likely to be used only as a gadfly breeding ground when summer came around.

Eleanor took up a stick and dragged it through the deep, still water. She collected an odd assortment of leaves and debris and deposited it carefully on the bank. It was an oddly childlike gesture, very like Will would make.

"I came to Potton before Will was born," she said, plunging the stick into the water again. "My husband and I were long estranged. It was obvious the baby was not his. My"—she paused as though she couldn't think of the word— "my relationship with Arthur was also over."

Caldwell could hear Will explaining in great detail his plans for the dam. Lady DeVaux, her skirts hiked up, had skipped across the rocks to join him on the plank at the top of the structure. DeVaux, sputtering cautions, looked as worried as Eleanor.

"Did Jordan know?" he asked. "About his cousin, I mean?"

"Yes."

No. This wasn't right. One couldn't change the facts in the middle of things. It confused everything, when he'd just started to make ordered sense of them. She had been Jordan's mistress and that relationship was done and that was that.

"So if it was obvious that the child was not Whitcombe's, why bother deceiving everyone that it was Jordan's child if it was not?" he asked. And what harm would it have done to confide the truth in him?

She appeared lost in thought for a moment. "I'm afraid it is a story that does not cast me in a very good light," she said at last. "When Arthur—well, when Arthur cast me off, I was frantic. Desperate. I was with child, and it would be obvious the baby was not my husband's, as everyone knew we kept separate homes. I was still very much in love with Arthur. He had taken up courting Miss Granville, Phoebe Granville, whom he later married." She stabbed the stick into the mud and made a series of holes. "I was just a castoff, nothing. I was furious. Maddened."

She tossed the stick into the woods and rubbed her arms as though she were cold.

"I wanted to publish his letters to me. To shame him. To let the world know what a horrid man he was. To show that I had been a decent, respectable woman before I met him. I didn't care how I blackened my own reputation so long as his name was blackened too."

She had loved Arthur DeVaux. Some rakish London swell he'd never met. He was surprised to find how much he hated the man.

"I knew Jordan through Arthur. Thank God he talked some sense into me," she went on. "He was the only friend I had. He helped me leave London, to let the house in Potton, to start a new life. He did everything."

Caldwell was having trouble assimilating all of this. Jordan was not the rogue of the story, he was the hero. The expression in her eyes proclaimed her eternal devotion to him. Reliable, dependable, wonderful Jordan DeVaux.

"Jordan insisted we keep his cousin's involvement with me a secret. For the sake of Arthur's reputation. There was talk in London for a while, of course. People knew Arthur and I had had a rather obvious flirtation. But he was soon married right and tight to Miss Granville, and I was gone." Eleanor turned and watched as DeVaux helped Phoebe and Will back across the brook.

He didn't like to think of Eleanor in love with Arthur DeVaux. One could hardly be jealous of a dead man, but oddly he found that he was. More, far more, than he had been of Jordan. It had been obvious that she did not feel romantically toward

Jordan. But Arthur? She had loved him. She had risked and lost everything for him.

Eleanor bent down to pick up a handful of stones and then threw them one by one into the water.

"That's the end of the story, really. I moved to Potton and began my life here. When Will was born, some people assumed he was Jordan's son. After all, he'd never made a secret of the fact that he'd helped me find the house here and was often about the place. Jordan didn't care what people said, and I, well, I suppose I found the gossip preferable to not having his friendship."

She stopped talking and was looking at him intently. Apparently he was supposed to react. But what to say?

"Why didn't you tell me?" It was not what he had meant to say, but that was all that was spinning in his brain.

"Jordan asked me not to tell anyone. He never wanted anyone to know the truth about Arthur. He'd rather he look like a cad than his cousin. I'm sorry I could not tell you earlier. Keeping that secret was the only thing Jordan ever asked of me. I had to do it."

Lord. Poor Phoebe. And Poor Eleanor. And poor Will. This was all more than he'd bargained for. With Eleanor, things were never simple.

She drew a slightly trembling breath and started to say something, then stopped again.

It didn't matter, of course. In fact, it made things easier. Jordan DeVaux was no longer a factor. The father of the child was dead. Eleanor was totally unattached.

But somehow this *did* change things. He wasn't sure she was who he'd thought she was. And worse, he wasn't certain he could measure up to Jordan's legacy. Or Arthur's. Or anyone's.

So he said nothing.

Eleanor turned to the others. "William, have you explained your project? I worry if we stay longer, Lady DeVaux will be chilled. We should not impose on her goodness too much, you know. And please button up your jacket, dear."

"Mama," Will said as he came over to her, "Lady DeVaux had some very good suggestions about my spillway. Do you think she could stay with us for a week as my engineering consultant?"

Eleanor smiled. "She may come as often and stay as long as she likes. I do hope she will," she said loudly enough that Phoebe might hear. "But do not hound her, dearest—"

"Good," said Will, turning back to Lady DeVaux. "Now you must come and tell me what you think of the greenhouse Professor Caldwell and I are building. And of course there is the fort. Normally we would not let civilians enter, but I might make an exception, since I am the commander."

Caldwell watched as she laughed after her son. Behind her good humor, though, she looked a bit tired. She'd had a lot to deal with of late. She turned back to him. "I've said my piece," she said with a wry smile. "Now, you said this morning that you had something you wished to discuss?"

"Oh." His mind was loose, flapping like an unmoored sail. He wasn't certain what to think. Why, why couldn't anything be simple? "Nothing," he said at last. "It wasn't important."

Chapter Sixteen

"Like this?" Will swung his pole wildly, nearly catching the fishhook in John's lapel, and ended up with the line merely plopping into the River Cam almost directly beside the boat.

"Excellent," said Caldwell. "See, you've done exactly the opposite of what the fish will expect. Highly strategic." The poor lad had never been fishing in his life before. It gave him an unexpected sense of pride that the boy would always recall today.

"So what do we do now?"

"Wait."

"Wait?" Will looked dismayed. "I'm not very good at waiting." He contemplated his hook and rod for a moment. "There must be a better way to do this. You can only catch one fish at a time. That's not very practical."

"My dear boy." Caldwell tilted his hat off his eyes enough to give Will a grin. "The purpose of fishing is not the fish, but the ing. It is the process, not the result, that is enjoyable."

Will waited for a moment, then leaned back and tilted his own hat over his eyes in a careful imitation of his mentor. "Can't really see the point," he said at last.

"You, sir, are exactly like your mother. Entirely unable to see the value of doing nothing."

Will crossed his arms across his narrow chest and looked determined to relax.

"How is your mother, by the way?" Caldwell asked.

"She's fine. She's always fine. I don't know why you always ask." The boy gave an exaggerated shrug.

"Because it's polite."

"But you ask it in that odd voice."

Caldwell made a dismissive noise and a mental note to stop asking quite so often.

He watched the cork on Will's line wobble with the gentle current. "It's just that I haven't seen her in quite a while," he said. "Where is she today?"

"Oh, she's in Cambridge." William indicated the buildings of the town over his shoulder. "She dropped me off at Professor DeVaux's rooms at Trinity so he could take me to you."

"Avoiding me, eh?"

Will looked at him in confusion, apparently not registering the joke. "No, I don't think so. Today she was going to call on Lady DeVaux."

"At Jordan's sister's house?" That was surprising. He knew through his visits to William that Lady De-Vaux had spent a good deal of time in Potton, but Eleanor had never called on her in Cambridge, where she was staying at Jordan's sister's house. Mrs. Hartfield, good soul that she was, was still not able to put it out of her mind that Eleanor was a woman with a past. He hoped Eleanor would not be turned away at the door.

"I believe Lady DeVaux is going back to London," Will went on, his lower lip protruding. "I wish she wouldn't. I like her. But Mama said that she was."

Caldwell opened an eye. Odd. He'd rather thought DeVaux had been courting her. Perhaps she'd given him the brush.

It was rather a consolation to think that DeVaux might be feeling the same way he was.

"Do you think Mama will get married again?" William asked suddenly, as though his own thoughts had wandered along the same path.

John closed his eyes and composed his features. Dashed warm today. Made it hard to relax. "I don't know. I suppose that's up to her."

He could hardly tell the boy that he had been on the brink of proposing to his mother himself. Not that she'd likely have said yes. After all, as she'd told him herself, she did not wish to be anyone's. And now that he knew the truth of her tumultuous relationship with Arthur DeVaux, he couldn't really blame her.

After a bit of mulling it over, he understood better why she had kept the secret of Will's paternity from him. Or rather, why DeVaux had insisted that the secret be kept. It was obvious now that Jordan had always been in love with Phoebe, even to the point of covering up for her philandering husband. But still. Eleanor might have trusted him.

"I always thought Mama might marry Professor DeVaux."

Caldwell opened one eye again and looked at the boy. "I always did too," he confessed.

Will gave a sage nod. "After all, they've known each other for a thousand years. I suppose they might as well."

He opened the other eye. "Might as well?"

The boy looked surprised. "Well, they are both rather old. But I suppose even old people would wish to marry."

Caldwell stifled the urge to laugh. "I suppose so."

"Well," Will continued serenely, "I daresay they won't. I should rather think Professor DeVaux would wish to marry Lady Phoebe DeVaux. After all, she is very pretty and lively. And she would be spared the trouble of changing her last name." He idly swung the rod back and forth. "I don't think I will ever marry. It seems to be a great deal of trouble."

Caldwell tilted his hat farther over his eyes. "You might feel different if you were in love."

"Love!" Will exclaimed with eight-year-old scorn. "I love the pony that Professor DeVaux gave me. I love cake. I love building things. I don't love girls."

"You love your mother," he pointed out.

"Of course. She's different."

"Yes," he said quietly after a moment. "She is." He contemplated the inside of his hat. "How would you feel if *I* married your mother?" he asked at last. "Just theoretically."

He hadn't been able to ask her the day Phoebe DeVaux visited. He'd been piqued and out of temper. But the idea had not let him rest. He realized now that it had nothing to do with practicality or logic or some philanthropic notion that he would graciously step in and save her reputation in the eyes of the world. It was because, dash it all, he'd somehow managed to fall in love with the woman.

For a worrying moment there was silence. "That would be all right, I suppose," the boy said. "It would mean you could help me build the extension on the fort. And I could read your book on pirates whenever I liked."

"I don't have much to offer her," he said, feeling as though he were asking permission from Will in lieu of her father. "I don't have a title or any fortune to speak of."

Will shrugged. "I don't think she cares about that." He looked a bit bored with the subject. "You can ask her," he said.

It was, of course, as simple as that. Ask and find out. But he found he could not be so cavalier. There were solid, practical reasons she should consider marrying him. Reasons that did not depend on her being able to reciprocate his feelings. But what if she still could not stomach it?

For the first time in his life he actually found himself wishing he had a title and a fortune. Not that she likely did care about those things. But she deserved them.

Perhaps it was ridiculous to consider asking her. She'd said already that she didn't want to be anyone's. And if she did marry, surely she would choose better than a Cheapside nobody. Even if it was a Cheapside nobody who now realized he was hopelessly in love with her.

"If I promise not to knock anything over like last time, do you think we could find Lord Fuller and try to make gunpowder again? Mama doesn't have to—look, look!"

The fishing rod had leapt out of Will's hands and was bumping along the edge of the boat, pulled toward the stern by the taut line.

Distracted by his spiraling thoughts, Caldwell was tempted to catch the devilish thing up and cast it whole into the river. Instead he lunged for the rod and returned it to Will.

"There now, reel it in. Gently, careful. No, not quite so gently."

"Professor Caldwell!"

Caldwell's head jerked up. What the devil? Now?

"Lord Berring," he said, bowing slightly to the man on the bank. "I hope you will excuse us for a moment while we reel in this perfectly enormous fish. Careful now, Will, don't jerk the line. Pull it in smoothly."

"Caldwell, what are you doing?"

He would have assumed that it was obvious to the Master both by their current activities and the fact that he had just a moment before explained what they were doing.

"Just a moment, sir. Now a bit more. Don't . . . not too—"

"Oh." Will looked devastated as the line suddenly went slack and his reel spun easily. "What happened?"

"Line broke. I'm afraid your whale got away. Sometimes they're too clever for us anglers." With a feeling of dread seeping into his bones, Caldwell took up the oars and rowed them closer to where the Master stood on the bank, his black gowns billowing like some unholy specter.

"What are you doing?" the man asked again.

"Sitting in a boat."

"And do you think that sitting in a boat is an appropriate pastime for a Trinity professor?"

"It's Saturday, sir."

This apparently was not the correct reply. The man's lips narrowed until they disappeared.

"When you are at Cambridge, sirrah, you are a professor, a representative of the university. I expect you to act like one."

"I'll keep that in mind in the future, sir."

"And who"—the Master fixed Will with a cold eye—"is this person?"

"William Whitcombe," Will said calmly.

"Whitcombe." The man's eyes narrowed. "The

notorious Lady Whitcombe's brat. So Whitcombe gave you his name, eh, boy? He didn't have anything else to do with your existence."

"I know," said Will. "But he did acknowledge me, so I am his heir."

Unable to discomfit the boy, the Master turned back to Caldwell. "I believe I told you, Caldwell, that I do not wish you to associate any longer with whores. Yes, I know both you and DeVaux go out to Potton all days of the week. I can fully imagine that Lady Whitcombe is very pleased to accommodate the both of you. After all, Dr. Stalk said the lady was accomplished in all manner of tricks of her trade."

"Sir." He tried to be calm. He tried to remember that the Master was only trying to provoke him. He gave the oars another push until the boat bumped into the bank, and then he stepped out on tight legs. "I must ask you not to speak that way of the lady. Particularly not in front of her son."

The Master's brows went up. "Don't tell me what I can or can't do, Professor. It is you who are breaching etiquette. If you must have a tumble, go to one of the tavern wenches or a brothel if you must. Lord knows I put up with DeVaux keeping the woman as a mistress. At least he, as a gentleman, knew how to be discreet."

"Sir, I must insist that we not have this conversation here."

Berring gave him a look of disgust. "You, however, with the smell of the shop still strong on you, can't help but consort most obviously with lower orders and fallen women. Picnics with students. Star-watching parties with townsfolk. A lazy job mentoring and too lenient by half. And now to top it off, despite my repeated warnings to stop seeing that woman, you insist on traipsing up to Potton like a dog after a bitch in heat."

Caldwell drew a shallow breath. In another moment he would boil over and there would be a disaster. "Sir, for the boy's sake . . . For everyone's sake, I really must insist—"

"She may call herself a lady, but I can assure you in London it was well known that she was on her back with a man not her husband."

"Sir—" Caldwell waited for the man to look up before he punched him in the jaw. "Go to hell."

There was a very satisfying splash as the man went into the river.

William clung to the bow, wide eyed, while the boat tossed in the tremendous wave that swallowed the Master. The bubble of the man's gown burbled at the surface for a moment, then went under as well. After a silent second or two, the Master came up again, sputtering incoherent profanities.

"Come on, Will." Caldwell reached down a hand to the boy and helped him out of the boat. They watched the Master wallow, unable in his heavy, wet robes to drag himself more than halfway out of the water. He looked rather like an emaciated seal, lolling and flopping on the bank. The man really did know a remarkable number of curses. Caldwell turned to go.

"Well," said Will after they had walked along the road in silence for a while. "That was a good deal more exciting than fishing."

Chapter Seventeen

Mrs. Agby put down the book from which she had been reading aloud and sighed. "Sacrifice for the common good," she said. "I cannot imagine anything more noble. It makes one nearly wish one were a man that one might have the honor of making such a sacrifice."

Eleanor took a sip of tea. "Why should one have to be a man?" she asked. "Is honor only a male trait? Is duty?"

Miss Jennings looked up, startled. "Yes, but it is so much more ordinary what is required of a woman. Obey your parents, then someday your husband. That is all." She looked around at the ladies of the Literary Society gathered in Lady Reed's drawing room for their approval.

"Yes," Eleanor said slowly. "But what if the choice became more difficult? What if your duty and your sense of right conflicted? For instance, what if your mother forbade you to come to the Literary Society? Hardly a moral imperative to attend, but I know you feel strongly that it is important for your education."

"I—I—" Miss Jennings looked very confused. "I suppose I would not go. But then again, to miss out

on the education of hearing our readings . . . " She
wrung her hands miserably.

"I would very much have liked to have bought a
new bonnet last week," Mrs. Gregory mused, "but
I felt it was my duty to refrain, as Mr. Gregory said
any more new bonnets this season and he would
feel obliged to start wearing them himself, so as to
ensure they were worn even once before they went
out of fashion."

"I often wonder," Eleanor said, almost to herself,
"if I am doing what is right by going against my in-
clinations. After all, it is indeed my inclination and
my selfish desires that have so often led me astray."
She looked around her circle of friends. "But were
I to always go against my desires, would I therefore
necessarily have been doing right? Fulfilling my responsibilities?"

"I don't think you would do wrong, Lady Whitcombe," Miss Jennings said reverently. "You seem to
always know what is good and right. At least"—she
added with a furious blush—"at least now."

Eleanor shook her head. If the ladies knew her
inclination, the temptation she'd faced from her
own overly passionate nature, even in the last few
months—well, especially in the last few months—
they should have a very different opinion of her
indeed. And, truth to be told, she rather wished
she'd been tempted more.

"I know someone who has made a great sacrifice
in order to do right," Miss Jennings said thoughtfully. "I do not know if it was against his inclination
or not, but I do indeed think it was a sacrifice to
duty and a moral responsibility." She smiled with a
look of romantic admiration. "He defended the
honor of a lady and in consequence lost everything."

"Who?" Lady Reed demanded. "And was it a sacrifice for love or indeed for duty?"

"Oh, duty, I should think," Miss Jennings replied. "For I don't believe—that is, I don't know. But the lady, I believe, was not all of the question. The gentleman had been grossly misused at the university, unjustly criticized and forced to do far more work than anyone else. But of course, because he was not a man of independent means, he could not leave. But he stood up for what was right for the sake of justice, and now he has lost his position."

"A university man?" Eleanor asked with sudden interest.

"Yes." Miss Jennings looked saddened. "That amiable Professor Caldwell who gave the lecture on stars."

"Professor Caldwell?" Eleanor exclaimed. "Lost his position at the university?"

Lady Reed clicked her tongue against her teeth. "Such a worthy man. I used to think him a bit irresponsible, but I do declare he has dined with us twice since the winter, when often before he would prefer to be in a tavern or a gaming salon. Even Mrs. Hartfield says he has been a good influence over her brother, Professor DeVaux. And I know she used to despair of the effects of their friendship."

"Professor Caldwell lost his position?" Eleanor said again, unable to believe it was true.

"And one must wonder though—his improvement aside—if this is what is truly meant by sacrifice for duty," Lady Reed went on. "Was his duty to stay on at the university despite the fact that he was ill used? Or was it his duty to leave? His inclination must have been to leave—"

"But now he shall have nothing," Miss Jennings said. "My papa says he was right to do it. He said that exposing the Master so fully by being unjustly dismissed will cause such a furor that it will provoke an examination of the system and prevent others from experiencing such tyranny."

"When did this happen? What will he do now?" Eleanor looked around at their blank, surprised faces and realized she was acting far more distraught than she ought.

"Only yesterday, I believe," Miss Jennings replied. "Papa said so at dinner. He was on the committee that the Master went to to get Professor Caldwell removed. They voted against it, you know. By seven to three. They say he is an excellent teacher and researcher, though he is, indeed, considered a bit wild. But by the time the deliberation was over, Professor Caldwell had tendered his resignation."

Eleanor put her teacup back onto the table, alarmed to see it rattle with her trembling hand. "Is that really the hour chiming?" she asked, her voice unnaturally high. "I'm afraid I must take my leave. William is still quite weak, you know, and I hate to leave him in Jenny's care for long."

She kept up a steady stream of prattle as she put on her spencer. "I do hope Lady DeVaux is able to join us next week. She has decided to stay in Cambridge after all, I believe. Goodness no, I couldn't possibly take any cake with me. I must run along directly. No, no, although you're very kind to offer, I am quite happy enough walking."

She made a rather hasty exit and was panting in the most undignified manner by the time the cottage came into sight. From the rise in the road she could see William carefully walking lengths on the ground by the vegetable patch.

She was surprised to see none other than Professor Caldwell himself following obediently behind the boy, noting things in his notebook. Had he really resigned from the university? Impossible. There was nothing that suited him better; he was so passionate about his work. Perhaps Miss Jennings was mistaken. She must be mistaken.

She lay down her reticule on the table in the hallway, finding herself suddenly a little afraid to go out to them. Ever since Will's illness things had been rather strained between her and Caldwell. And then, when the truth about Arthur came out . . .

She went through the silent house and stood in the back doorway.

"I should think this will do very well," Caldwell was saying. "The sweet peas will go here, against the wall, and there, in the morning sun, the snapdragons."

"Mama." Will looked up in surprise. "You have come home far too early. We were planning a surprise for you."

"For me?" She could see now that they had extended the vegetable patch several yards, carefully lined it with round stones, and tilled the earth for planting.

"We are making you a flower garden. It will be a very small one, to be sure. But Professor Caldwell said that everyone should have some bit of garden for nothing but beauty. So we are planning one for you."

"How thoughtful," she said, her throat very tight. "I have missed having a flower garden."

William looked so pleased, she hoped she did not disgrace herself by suddenly bursting into tears.

Caldwell's grave look disconcerted her still more. To avoid complete disaster, she muttered something about tea and fled into the kitchen. The steam was rattling the top of the kettle before she felt somewhat more contained.

Caldwell had resigned from his position at Trinity. If it were true then he would leave Cambridge.

The kitchen door opened and Caldwell himself came in.

"Your son has sent me to plead on his behalf that Jenny's seedcake be added to the tea tray."

"Ah, of course." She whirled around and swept up the entire section that was left, to deposit it unceremoniously onto the tray.

"How was the Literary Society meeting?" he asked politely.

She turned to take the kettle off the fire, but he was there before her. "Oh dear me, I can take the kettle myself. There's no need, well, thank you." He was standing far too close, but she was somehow unable to move away. "John," she burst out, "is it true? Have you resigned from Trinity?"

His brows went up slightly. "How news travels. Was it William who told you?"

"Will?" she exclaimed in bewilderment. "He knew? Then it is true?" She knew by his silence that it was. "But why?"

He took up the tea tray and carried it out to the small iron table in the garden. "I have thought for a long time that there was a misalliance between myself and Trinity," he said at last. "Or at least Trinity in its current reign."

She looked at him for a long moment, waiting for the rest, but he did not go on.

William bounded over with a squeak of pleasure at seeing such a large chunk of seedcake.

"When you see the garden, Mama, you must appear very surprised. It is only right when you came home unexpectedly." He positioned the knife over a rather significant percentage of the cake.

"William," Eleanor said gravely, moving the knife to a more reasonable place on the cake, "what do you know about Professor Caldwell's leaving his position at the university?"

She had the thin satisfaction of seeing both Will and Caldwell give a guilty start.

"The Master said unkind things about you," William said at last with a reluctant wiggle. "We saw him at the river when we went fishing yesterday. He's an awful man, Mama. All nose and upper lip. I wanted to hit him, so I was very glad when Professor Caldwell did."

"Hit him?" she gasped. "Defending *me*?"

Will's eyes were gleaming in admiration. "Whump, just like that!" He did a reenactment. "Just like a Barbary pirate. And the Master fell in the river." He demonstrated this with enthusiasm.

"What? Is this true?"

Caldwell gave a sigh. "Of course, it was a very impulsive and wrong thing to do. Violence is never an appropriate response. And that isn't the whole of the reason I'm going. The Master has wished me gone for a long while now. I've simply decided to oblige him." He spoke lightly, but there were grim lines around his mouth.

"I cannot believe you wish to go," she said. "You have always said that Trinity was the best place for astronomers. You scorned other colleges and other universities."

His laugh had a hollow ring. "It is the best. Perhaps that's why I never fit in. I'm too cocky by half, and perhaps I don't have enough to back it up."

"Nonsense. I know how hard you work."

He gave a shrug. "My renewed efforts were perhaps too late. Ah well, I've been offered a position at St. John's. Though I doubt I shall stay at Cambridge. Perhaps something will come up elsewhere. I've a fancy for Ireland at times. Perhaps I could go up to Dublin."

Unsure of what to say, she sat down and poured the tea. William looked from one of them to the other. Then, deciding neither was going to reprimand him for either telling or not telling yesterday's events, he got up off the grass and happily tucked into the seedcake.

Eleanor had almost gotten used to not feeling guilty. But now it all came back in a rush. "This is my fault. I should have seen, after how he acted at the Easter Term Ball—"

"No." Caldwell took her hand and pressed it. He likely hadn't noticed he'd done it; the gesture was so natural. "I only wish, well, I only wish it had done some good." He smiled. "Brutishly hitting a man is hardly likely to change his opinions." His forefinger was making tiny circles on the top of her hand. "I only wish that he was not such an ignorant boob that he deserved a hiding."

Caldwell couldn't leave. He just couldn't. "I don't want you to go. That is, Will and I . . ."

His hazel eyes were steady on hers. He seemed to be waiting, tense. She cleared her throat. "We have done a disservice to your career by allowing you to befriend us so kindly. It has been selfish of us."

He turned away. "Nonsense. It is the wrong way around. I have let you down as a friend many times. But I hope I now know your value. I hope someday I can make you believe how very dear I hold this connection."

She said nothing, unable to speak. He was so

rarely serious. When he was, the effect was shattering.

Caldwell released her hand and turned to Will. "Very well, William. I'm afraid I must take my leave. If I cannot come to help you finish the flower garden, I'll send the plans with DeVaux. He'll know what to do."

Will's face was growing pinched, so Eleanor decided that their parting was perhaps a private thing. She left her tea cooling on the table and went toward the house, murmuring something about getting his coat and hat and ringing for his horse from the new groom DeVaux had hired to look after the pony Phoebe had badgered him to buy for Will.

She could not fall apart now. There was time enough for that later.

The hallway was dim and quiet. She leaned against the wall, her breath coming fast as though she had been running. She must be rational. She must not give in to passion or hysteria. She had cost him his position at the university. There was no reason to make things worse by embarrassing them both with sentimentality.

She had barely time to draw a few breaths before she heard his steps behind her. She helped him into his coat in silence, greedily touching his shoulders, elbows, any last contact.

"Tell me," she said at last, her voice embarrassingly hoarse. "Tell me this is not the—no, that is not right. What I mean to say is, if our friendship must end, please let it be because you are going on to do something you enjoy doing. I would feel so very consoled if I knew, after you were gone, that my loss was indeed your gain."

He was looking at her curiously. "So you are not made of stone after all," he said softly.

He took her chin in his hands and looked down at her. She wanted to pull away, to hide the fact that the tears in her eyes would spill over any moment and she would be bawling like a fool.

"You must not blame yourself for this," he said. "Despite my dramatic scene with the Master yesterday, my troubles at the university had nothing to do with you. Do you understand?"

She nodded like a child, unable to speak.

She could hear his horse's hooves crunching on the drive outside as the groom brought the animal around. In another moment John would be gone.

"I should have told you sooner about Will's father," she blurted. "I should not have kept such a secret from someone who has been so good to us. I hope that is not why"—her voice was not working properly, squeaking and choking like a rusty pump—"why you have been so distant of late."

At that point, of course, the tears did flood over. But she didn't really care anymore.

"Oh Eleanor, you lovely widgeon," he said, just like the old Caldwell. He drew out a handkerchief and dried her eyes for her, as though she couldn't very well do it herself.

"I don't give a red damn who Will's father was. Or any of the details of your past. If I've been distant, well, it was because I realized when Will was ill and I didn't come to you that I had been the most unreliable of men. I was resolved to show you I'd changed. I wanted you to know that I was trustworthy. Dependable. Lord, I wanted so much to—well, no matter now. I've no prospects to offer any woman now."

He shoved his hands into his trouser pockets in the boyish gesture she'd grown to love.

She could hear the horse outside growing restless. This was the end.

"I must go," he said unnecessarily. He abruptly shoved a hand out to her. "Thank you, Lady Whitcombe. No matter where I end up, I'll remember . . ."

She took his hand to shake it. Only a few more moments and he would be gone. Then she could fall apart. Then she could be heartbroken. He looked down at their clasped hands and said nothing.

"No," he said hoarsely at last. "This won't do." He leaned forward and kissed her lightly on the lips.

All the things left to say crowded into her throat and threatened to choke her. Lord, in another moment she would be a total watering pot. She just stood there, stupid, staring into his eyes.

He must have read her plea in her eyes, for he kissed her again, this time a real kiss, his arms going tightly around her, his mouth slanting over hers. It was like that first kiss under the shooting stars, but this time there was tenderness. As though, more than wanting her, he cared for her. He kissed her as a man would kiss a woman he was courting. With fervency, urgency, but not with lust. She had never been touched like that.

Strangely, it was the pleasure, the painful sweetness, of his kiss that made her break it at last. Lust she understood. Desire. She felt it now. But this new tenderness, now when he was leaving, was too painful.

She pulled away from him and drew a deep breath. She could not look him in the face knowing it would be for the last time. So she merely leaned her forehead against his chest, as she had always wished to do, and for a moment inhaled the scent of him.

"I wanted to ask you—"

She looked up at him, holding her breath. "Yes?"

He shook his head with a grim look. "It's nothing. No. Just . . . just think of me, occasionally. Perhaps when you see a falling star." He made a comical face. "Or whenever you meet an arrogant, difficult man with a chip on his shoulder about his birth and too much pride to know what's good for him."

"I will think of you," she said softly.

He caught her chin in his hand as though he would kiss her again, but he did not. Instead he merely looked at her face, gravely intent, studying her.

"Good-bye," he said at last.

"Yes." She opened the door. There was no point in saying what should not be said. There was no point in telling him she loved him. It would only complicate things, and Caldwell, she well knew, hated complication.

Instead she turned up her mouth in a smile she knew was not the least bit believable. "Good-bye."

Chapter Eighteen

"I'm sorry, madam." The clerk did not look terribly sorry. "But the Master is a very busy man. He is meeting with the council right now, and I cannot say when he will be back. Even then, he likely will not be able to talk with you."

Still perched at his high desk, he opened up a ledger book and dipped his quill in his pot of ink with an expression of bored finality. "Perhaps we could set an appointment. I'm afraid the Master is not available until next month. He is a very busy man. But I believe he could set aside perhaps ten minutes for you on the twentieth."

After a moment, he looked up with an expression of surprise, as though he hadn't expected to find her still there.

"What is the matter regarding? Your son's admission, perhaps? I have to warn you that the Master does not take well to personal pleas for favors from people without means. You must apply in the regular way."

Eleanor gave him a sweet smile. "It isn't about college admissions. And I cannot wait until next month. It will have to be today. I will wait here until the Master returns. I do believe he will see me."

She lowered her lids slightly and allowed her lips

to curl up at the corners in imitation of the old, indiscreet Eleanor. The man looked stunned and muttered a few half sentences.

She turned to the window and watched the students in the courtyard. How peculiar it was to see them all dressed the same, trundling about like ants. One figure in ornate robes swept through their ranks. The students parted and seemed suddenly in a great bustle to get where they were going.

"There he is," she said pleasantly. "I'll just go down and meet him. I don't believe my interview will take very long."

The clerk sputtered his protests and actually rose up as though he would race across the room and block the door, but she ran lightly down the stairs and into the fresh dampness of the Great Court.

It was an imposing square of gray stone, carved and turreted in the heavy Tudor style. On all four sides it was closed in with monumental buildings: its ponderous gatehouse, solemn chapel, and of course, in a place of ceremony next to the Great Hall, the imposing hulk of the Master's Lodge. Overall, the Court was designed to strike awe in the hearts of those who were not a part of its academic machinery.

But today, with the bright spring breeze playfully spattering the water from the basin of the central fountain and the grass of the court looking green and springy enough to roll on, it was hard to feel too intimidated.

The Master was absorbed in swishing his gown in the grandest manner and glowering at a set of students who were skylarking on the lawns. He drew up short when she did not move out of his way.

"What is this?" He looked surprised, then furious.

"Who let you in here? I'm afraid, madam, you must leave before I call the porters on you. Trinity is a male establishment. Respectable males."

"Yes, yes, and I am neither," she said cheerfully. "And I would of course be happy to leave, if you could just set my mind at ease about something."

"Your mind at ease?" he echoed scornfully. "Lady Whitcombe, your title will not protect you here. I'm afraid I'm only too aware of how little a true gentlewoman you are. And if you've come to plead the case of your current paramour, Professor Caldwell, I'm afraid you're too late. He has already resigned."

"Indeed?" She gave a dismissive shrug. "A pity. My dear friend Lady DeVaux was just telling me the other day that there are no fewer than three extremely wealthy patrons who were very interested in contributing to Trinity due to Caldwell's work on star formation. I daresay the money will go with him wherever he goes."

"Nonsense. You don't know what you are about."

He started in visible repulsion when she slipped her arm through his. "Oh, indeed I do. As you must know, Lady DeVaux and I both have a great many connections in London. And the Classics Society alone is prepared to make a reasonable endowment. You know Lady Reed is such a devotee of Caldwell's work."

All true, actually. Phoebe, it turned out, had a genuine talent for convincing people to part with their money for academic causes.

"Your connections in London," he sniffed. "I know all about your connections. Cast-off wife and cast-off mistress. Now you're nothing but a poor widow with neither money nor reputation to your name."

"Mmmm," she murmured, pulling him along the

sunny walk. "Isn't the sunshine lovely? It really has been a remarkably warm spring. You know, Lord Berring"—she stopped and looked him full in the face—"the consequence of being a cast-off wife and cast-off mistress is that one does make the acquaintance of a great many other castoffs as well. Oh, do mind the puddle, sir. Italian leather shoes are so difficult to clean once they are wet.

"And I did happen to learn of some of *your* castoffs," she went on with a smile. "There is a young lady employed as a maid in Sir Bentford Jennings' house who I was interested to hear bears a great resemblance to you. Though much more handsome, of course. You know Sir Bentford, of course, as he is on the dean's committee. His daughter is in the Ladies' Literary Society."

His joints tightened. "I don't know what you're—"

"Indeed, though perhaps happily for her, her disposition is more like her mother's. I spoke with Mrs. Grady yesterday. We cast-off women do love to commiserate, you know. And what is truly remarkable is that Miss Grady is your daughter. Now of course I would hate to shock you with a revelation like that if I thought you didn't know, but Mrs. Grady assured me that she had petitioned you many times for support."

"Lying jade," the man exclaimed. "She could never prove the brat was mine."

Eleanor gave a throaty laugh. Ah, she felt like the old Eleanor again. Confident, brash, and determined to get just what she wanted. "Yes, these things are most abominably difficult. But have you seen the young lady? I'm afraid there is no doubt of her parentage." She gave a critical glance down his narrow length, from his thin nose to his angular feet.

"Now, to continue with my story, if you'll indulge me, Miss Grady, a really lovely girl, I'm pleased to say, is employed, along with her mother, in the household of Sir Bentford. I believe her mother was fortunate enough to find employment there after you discharged her? Lord, but she had any number of stories to tell. I had no idea you supplemented your income in so many creative ways when it came to taking bribes for degrees. You naughty man. How lucky you are that Mrs. Grady has been so discreet. Up to now, I mean."

She was very satisfied to see the way the Master gave a start and stopped right in the middle of a rather muddy puddle. "Damn you. Damn all of you. Sir Bentford Jennings should mind his own business."

She gave him her most innocent smile. "Such an odd thing how everyone in the world is connected. You wouldn't have thought such an unsavory sort as me would be so closely linked with people like you."

"You are attempting to blackmail me," the Master burst out, his face going an odd purple.

"Blackmail you?"

"You imply that if I do not give your precious Caldwell his job back, you will intercede with Sir Bentford to expose that . . . that girl, my past. . . ." He made a gesture as though to push away all those unsavory things.

She lifted her shoulders. "Good Lord, no. It cannot be a threat, for Sir Bentford has already gone to the council about it. Such a stickler about hypocrisy, you know. And I really only mentioned at dinner last night—Miss Jennings is kind enough to ask me to dinner quite often, you see—that his maid resembled you. Then Sir Bentford ferreted out the whole. He's quite the Bow Street Runner once he gets an idea into his head."

She listened to the Master sputter for a moment.

"I merely wished to tell you, so that you might do your utmost to convince Caldwell to return. After all, the council is planning on investigating this affair quite closely. They can't have their best professors just resigning willy-nilly of course. And I'm a bit afraid you might come off the worse for it.

"I know, of course, that your position is a crown appointment," she went on thoughtfully. "But Sir Bentford felt strongly that the King might wish to reconsider his choice if he knew the circumstances. However outrageously the Prince might behave, the King is *very* concerned with propriety."

The Master stared at her for a moment, his expression one of loathing. "You . . . you . . . *harlot.*"

"I thank you. I can see that you were thinking of a rather worse word than that. Well, perhaps it shows that you do appreciate my warning you after all. I can't say that your efforts will do any good. After all, Caldwell is a stubborn and proud man. And the committee is not entirely certain that his staying on or going would affect your fate at all.

"But of course, were he to stay and were those lovely endowments to come in, I suspect that the committee would be a great deal closer to pacified."

"I will not stoop to being manipulated," he growled, but Eleanor could see his fingers twitching.

She released his arm. "Of course not. I know you are a man who makes rational decisions based on factual circumstances." She looked up at the clock tower. "Oh dear me, I've taken up a great deal too much of your time. How cross your clerk will be with me. Well, now that you are in possession of the facts, I shall leave you to consider them."

She did not offer her hand, knowing that he would not shake it, but instead made a civil bow and wished him an exceedingly cheerful good morning.

Chapter Nineteen

DeVaux walked into Caldwell's chambers without knocking, his usual taciturn humor veneered with smugness.

Caldwell gave him a pained look and threw another set of books into the trunk. "You're smelling of April and May," he said irritably. "I suppose that means Lady DeVaux has decided not to leave Cambridge?"

"She did leave," DeVaux said. "But she came back." He removed a stack of shirts from the leather wing chair and dropped into it with an entirely satisfied sigh. "Yes, things are going very well indeed."

It was a bit unfeeling of his friend to appear so pleased when he was leaving. Leaving everything: the university, William, Eleanor. The idea of going back to his parents' plain, respectable home on Moorgate Road was more than demoralizing. It was humiliating. He'd failed. "I suppose you'll marry her."

Jordan leaned back and grinned, flushed as a schoolboy. "I suppose I will."

People in love were so very selfish. Never even considered what other people might be feeling. "Caught in the parson's mousetrap," he said with a laugh that didn't come out sounding right. "I never thought it would happen to you. Though I daresay a man of your breeding is obliged to marry. Had to happen at some point. And of course Lady DeVaux is a very good sort."

"High praise indeed," Jordan said with a laugh. "In fact, I shall take it as an admission that she is the most beautiful, admirable, adorable, perfect woman on earth."

Caldwell had always rather liked Phoebe, and he knew he should be pleased that his best friend was happy. But of course, married people didn't keep in touch with their bachelor friends anymore. Certainly not when their bachelor friends were leaving in disgrace to God knew where.

"You shouldn't pack," DeVaux said suddenly, noticing what he was doing.

"Why not? There's no one else to do it."

His friend stretched languorously and then pillowed his arms behind his head. "The committee has not decided you should go."

Caldwell sorted through some correspondence, then impatiently dropped it all into the trunk. "I have decided I should go. I lost my temper and behaved abominably. And worse, I put up with the Master's insufferable petty insults for far too long. No, Cambridge is not the right place for me."

He turned and went to put his violin back into its case. He'd been tempted to spend the afternoon playing maudlin tunes to match his mood, but Berwild had banged on the wall and shouted, so he'd been forced to content himself with staring moodily out the window and occasionally tossing something into his trunks.

DeVaux drew out a letter from his pocket. "Jennings asked me to deliver this to you. It is from the committee. They request that you stay."

"Stay? They request that I stay?" His brain stopped for a moment, unsure how to move on. "I've resigned. I can't stay." The strange, out-of-control feeling was starting again.

"Nonetheless, I believe they do request it. But you'll have to read it yourself." DeVaux propped his legs on a bust of Nicolaus Copernicus, watching while Caldwell broke the seal on the letter. "The Master resigned, you know," he said mildly.

"What?" John looked up from the tidy script of the letter. "He what?"

"Resigned. Heard Sir Bentford Jennings pressured him." DeVaux caught sight of a book and took it up with interest. "I believe this book is mine. I loaned it to you some time ago. Do you mind if I—yes, see, here is my name. God knows what else you were intending to steal. I'll have to search your trunks."

"Take it. Please. Take them all. I don't care. Now what is this about the Master resigning?"

"If this keeps up, there will be no one left at Trinity." DeVaux moved the book into the slanting shaft of late-afternoon sunlight and continued to read. A small quirk to his mouth indicated that he was well aware he was being irritating.

"There's been talk of it for some time, you know," DeVaux said at last. "Recent events effectually put the nail in the coffin. Likely an investigation of why you resigned after popping him into the river would have turned up more than he liked. He's going back to Oxford to head their Archives and Antiquities department." DeVaux allowed himself a genuine smile. "Quite a step down."

"And they want me to stay," Caldwell said in wonderment. The letter said so. The Dean, in his tortuously pompous way, said so.

"Of course they do. You're the best they have."

"Besides you."

DeVaux shrugged. "I hope you'll stay."

He was all at sea. Ten minutes ago he knew what was what in his life. He wasn't happy about it, but he knew everything was a direct result of his decisions. This, however, made no sense. He continued to stare at the letter. "There is a fine for striking my superior. But it is only five pounds." He looked up at DeVaux. "Why are they doing this?"

"You'll stay?"

He didn't know what to say. This changed everything. Unexpectedly, he found he urgently wanted Eleanor's advice. He pushed down the lid of the trunk and sat on it. This opened a thousand possibilities.

"I heard," said DeVaux, opening another book and looking over its contents, "that Lady Whitcombe was seen in peculiar company this morning."

This snapped him back to reality. "Peculiar company?" he echoed.

"Boxty saw her within the court with the Master." He jerked his head toward the mullioned window facing Trinity's Great Court.

"The—"

"You've got in the dreadful habit of repeating things these days," DeVaux said with an indulgent smile. "I don't know what passed between them, but it must have been monumental. Jennings said the man tendered his resignation but a few hours later."

What the devil? How could she have done it?

He was dragging on his coat before he knew what he was about.

"I take it you are staying?" DeVaux said, looking up as he closed the book.

Caldwell attempted to cram his hat on his head, draw out his watch, and button his coat simultaneously. Then he stopped for a moment and grinned.

"May I borrow five pounds?"

Chapter Twenty

Caldwell bolted down the stairs, suddenly desperate to get to Potton. If nothing else, he needed to find out what she had done to effect the Master's departure.

No, no, that wasn't it. Truth to be told, he didn't give a hang about the Master or how she'd done it. He was well aware that Eleanor could make a man do all kinds of mad things.

He needed to get to Potton to ask her to marry him. Beg, plead, rationalize, lecture—whatever it took. He should have done it long ago if he hadn't been so damned proud.

"Caldwell!" Chesterfield came around the corner at the bottom of the stone stairs. "I heard the news. You're staying? I thought you would. Very good, very good. Can't imagine what we would have done without you. Though of course I did consider immediately claiming your time in the observatory. Otherwise that dog Berwild would have taken it for his ridiculous measurements of Saturn's rings. Hopelessly old-fashioned. Now, shall we have a drink? A coup like this deserves a little drink, wouldn't you say?"

Caldwell allowed the man to pump his arm

nearly out of its socket while he stammered his
thanks. "I really . . . I really must go—"

"Nonsense. Time enough for a drink. And here
is Hart. Hart, DeVaux, you must help me convince
Caldwell here to come to the combination room
for a sherry."

"No, really, I—"

"I believe today is the day that Mrs. Harris throws
her musical salon," DeVaux said mildly as he came
down the stairs. "Everyone you know in Potton will
be there. If you happen to be thinking about riding
there, you might do better to wait until tomorrow."

Chesterfield and Hart looked at him as though
he were babbling nonsense. Caldwell nodded
slowly, feeling dazed. He allowed himself to be
dragged to the somber, wood-paneled combination
room and managed to sit through a drink or two
while the gossip and speculation babbled over him.

Couldn't people understand that he really
could't care less about the Master's fall from grace
and the strange circumstances that surrounded it?
He was reinstated. He had a future. He had the
kind of prospects one could offer a wife.

He couldn't concentrate properly. He thought
he'd never sit in the great dining hall again, listening to the Latin prayers and complaints about the
food. He'd expected that it would be DeVaux or
Chesterfield who would be climbing the hill
tonight to be giving the outdoor night lecture on
orbit.

But life at the university went on in a strangely ordinary pattern, and in the evening after dinner he
found himself standing on his favorite hilltop
under a spill of familiar stars as he listened to the
soft, disgruntled mutterings of the group of stu-

dents trying to work out the problem he'd posed for them.

For once, the sky held no attraction for him. The stars were still and bright and predictably in their place. Regulus in Leo, Sirius in Canis Major, Rigel bright in Orion. The Hydra constellation snaking across the southern sky. Before, he'd always found them a comfort. Now, however, they seemed distant, passionless.

He kept being distracted by the lights of Cambridge, and farther—so much farther they were likely imaginary—the lights of a small town down the road.

He felt like a student the night before exams. By this time tomorrow it would all be over. He would know his answer. He would know if he had passed or failed.

He cut the lecture a bit short. He couldn't concentrate any further. It would be better to walk out his anxiety by the river, or count the stars alone in peace.

The boys gathered up their papers and books, suddenly a great deal more animated, and headed off toward the twinkling lights of the Three Tuns tavern.

Even Eckles, the eternal questioner, lingered only for a few minutes to ensure that he had gotten the answer to the assigned problem correct. For a dangerous moment, Caldwell thought he might actually offer to help him fold up the three repeating circles and transport them back to the observatory, but he too eventually trundled off down the hill.

Alone at last. Caldwell set about loosening the screws that stabilized the legs of the instruments. His mind, dulled by the continuous track of questions circling it since DeVaux's odd visit this afternoon, could focus on only one task at a time.

"May I disturb you?"

He looked up and saw Eleanor standing there in her gray cloak, almost invisible in the darkness. He started and then tried to cover it up, but found he'd dropped all the screws onto the grass. "Of course," he said, too loudly and too cheerfully. "I'm glad to see you, actually. I was going to come and see you tomorrow."

She seated herself on the exposed rock at the crest of the hill. "They've convinced you to stay then?" She leaned back on her hands and watched him scrabble for the lost screws. There was something new in her voice, even in the way she sat—a confidence, an almost laughing sensuality.

"Yes. That is, yes, thanks to you. I hear you went to see the Master." He found the last of the screws and sat back on his heels. "What did you say to make him resign?"

Her laugh was low in the darkness. "Even a woman like me has connections. My days in London society stood me well. As did my days as a social outcast. Let us just say that the Master, like everyone, has rather tarnished elements in his past." She looked up at him, those gray eyes more serious than ever. "I did not want you to go, John."

He cleared his tightening throat. Keep it light, keep it friendly. She'd never believe him trustworthy or responsible if he pounced on her every time he was alone with her. But Lord. He wanted nothing more than to take her into his arms, kiss her senseless, and babble the most sentimental of nonsense. He cast a quick glance to where she was sitting, leaning back on her arms, even the simple cut of her gown unable to disguise her remarkable figure or that pale, perfect skin.

"No," he said with a strained laugh. "I wasn't too keen to go either. Didn't really have a plan. It would have been—but it's late for you to be out, Eleanor. What brings you out here to Cambridge in the middle of the night? Will is well, I hope?"

"Very well." She was smiling at him in a peculiar way. "I came here to see you."

"It's a very long way. I planned to come see you tomorrow." He felt like a student who has suddenly learned that exam time is one day earlier than he thought. He was not prepared. He needed more time.

Her placid expression did not falter. "I'm afraid it could not wait."

"No?" With every appearance of nonchalance, he folded up the repeating circle and moved on to the next one. "Well, I'm glad you did come. I wanted to thank you. That is, it was very kind of you to use your influence. I'm not sure what the devil happened, but despite appearances, the position means a great deal to me."

"I didn't do it to be kind."

He clumsily pinched his fingers in his attempt to fold up the apparatus. "No?"

"I prefer to have you in debt to me," she laughed. "And I came to make you an offer."

His fingers stopped. "An offer?"

She had risen and come to stand over where he was crouched. She put her hand on her hip in a defiant gesture. "I would like to become your mistress."

He rose to his feet and stared at her. His mind was moving very slowly. "I thought you—"

"Yes," she said, "I vowed I would never be another

man's possession. And I will not." Her proud look was softened with a smile that was almost shy. "I do what I wish these days, John. And I find I wish to be with you."

He was speechless.

Her chin went up. "If you do not wish it, of course—"

"It isn't that I don't wish it," he said quickly. "God knows, I've desired you from the moment I saw you. But becoming my mistress will not answer."

A frown formed between her lovely brows. "Why not? We enjoy each other's company. We are attracted to each other. We are both rational adults. Why should society's notions impede us?"

He looked up at the sky, just to make certain it was still there. Yes, all in its place. The world hadn't tipped on its axis. "What impedes us is not society. It's me. I'm in love with you, Eleanor. And nothing by halves will do. I'm afraid you'll have to marry me."

His brain, a moment ago sluggish, was now dancing about in seven directions at once. She did care for him. She must. She would not have gone to so much trouble to ensure his position if she did not. She would not have offered the one thing she said she would never offer any man if she did not care.

"I know I don't have much to offer a woman like you," he said carefully. "I'm ill born, not near rich as you deserve. Devil take it, I only barely have a position here, but—"

"Marry you?" She looked up at him with a blank expression. "I can't."

"Why not?"

"It doesn't make any sense. I've offered to become your mistress. I've ceased to care what the world thinks of me. Why should we marry?"

He threw back his head and laughed. "Now you have brought it to a question of logic. You maddening, beautiful woman. Let's disprove the hypothesis. We should *not* marry because we are not matched in social station. Because I am a careless, cynical fellow, and you are a woman with a notorious past. There is no financial, social, moral, or logical reason we should marry." He took her face between his hands. "But it doesn't matter. I love you. And there are a thousand reasons to love you."

She said nothing, just stared at him with wide, bewildered eyes. He felt a squeeze of panic. There was no mistaking the attraction between them, but love? He could kiss her, arouse a passion in her that would make her accept his proposal, accept anything. But he wanted more than that. More than passion. Irrationally, illogically, and entirely, he wanted her.

"I have never been loved before," she said softly at last. "And while I knew lust and passion and obsession, I have never really loved anyone before either. I didn't know that loving someone and liking someone and desiring someone could all be focused on the same person." She shook her head, looking almost embarrassed. "It makes no sense."

In an instant she was in his arms, where she should have been long ago. "No," he said. "It makes no sense."

"No," she agreed, between kisses.

"Nor does marrying me, but you must do that as well."

She pulled back from him, just enough to look him full in the face. "Yes. If you like. Though I will doubtless make things quite complicated for you."

"I love complicated."

"Your family will not be pleased."

"Even better."

"And you know William will still be a peer. I'm afraid it cannot be helped."

"I shall strive to get over it."

She let him kiss her for a good deal longer. "Can you ever forget the fact that I am a fallen woman?" she asked, with a wicked gleam in her eyes.

"Will you be content to be dull, ordinary, respectably married Mrs. Caldwell?" he countered. When she nodded, he looked gravely into her eyes. "More important, could you learn to love me, Eleanor?"

She met his gaze, with a smile that told him yes. "Learn?" she echoed. "How can one learn these kinds of things? They do not come from the mind. I already know how to love you, John. I think I must have a natural genius."

He held her closer and kissed her again, pleased to feel her breath quicken. "I think we must marry very soon indeed," he said at last with a grin.

She looked quite flushed and breathless, but she nodded. "Though I'm afraid it will cause a great deal of talk."

"Excellent," he said. "I detest respectability."

BOOK YOUR PLACE ON OUR WEBSITE
AND MAKE THE
READING CONNECTION!

We've created a customized website just for our very
special readers, where you can get the inside scoop on
everything that's going on with Zebra, Pinnacle and
Kensington books.

When you come online, you'll have the exciting
opportunity to:

- View covers of upcoming books

- Read sample chapters

- Learn about our future publishing schedule
  (listed by publication month *and author*)

- Find out when your favorite authors will be visiting
  a city near you

- Search for and order backlist books from our
  online catalog

- Check out author bios and background information

- Send e-mail to your favorite authors

- Meet the Kensington staff online

- Join us in weekly chats with authors, readers and
  other guests

- Get writing guidelines

- AND MUCH MORE!

Visit our website at
http://www.kensingtonbooks.com

More Regency Romance
From Zebra